The Twelve Parties of Christmas

AMY OLIVEIRA

First e-book edition December 2020

Illustration by Ilustratam
Edited by Helena Bracken

www.amyoliveira.com

To my grandparents,

For the best Christmas meals of my life.

CHAPTER ONE

"It's not a big deal."

"You're right, it isn't."

"It's not like we are never going back."

"Exactly."

I opened the door an inch more to find Mam's frowning face looking at Emmet.

"Why aren't you freaking out?"

Emmet eyebrows shot up but he held back his smile, "Because isn't a big deal."

"Oh yeah, that's true."

The scene felt like Deja vu. Mam was overreacting and pacing the length of our apartment's sitting room while Emmet's voice remained calm and collected, answering her questions with nothing but logical thinking, though I could tell he was holding back a laugh.

I closed my bedroom door slowly, trying not to alarm them that I was eavesdropping. Again. But listen, I'm seventeen years old and there's so many things about my life that I am not authorized to decide myself. Like where we live, even though Mam brought me to every apartment they visit and asked my opinion. Or what school I should go to... Well, Emmet actually got brochures of the options and...

Look, every teenager eavesdrops on their parents. It's just something we do. If you know the information beforehand you can get yourself ready for whatever is coming. For example, Mam decided not to go back to Yellow Meadows for Christmas and now, thanks to eavesdropping, I could assess my feelings in the privacy of my room.

I sat on the bed where the fantasy book I was reading was still open. I was born and raised in Yellow Meadows, this tiny little town in Ireland. I love it there. It's kooky and weird, and honestly, the best people in the world are from Yellow Meadows. Plus it looks absolutely gorgeous during Christmas.

We always go back for the holidays, even those years when we left early to spend New Year's in New York. Christmas? That was Yellow Meadows' territory, it was never a question before, not at least from me.

I bit my cheek and sighed. In my minds' eye I could see it perfectly, Yellow Meadows' Main Street lit up with the big colourful lights, and the big luscious Christmas tree in the middle of the square. The delicious smell of freshly baked cookies from the Christmas Fair...

Well, apparently those times were over now. Mam married Emmet Scott, (Yes, yes, THE Emmet Scott.) and we had moved to New York almost five years ago.

God. Five years ago. It had never occurred to me that my memories of Yellow Meadows are all from when I was a child. I got my first kiss in New York and my first boyfriend too. I barely talked to my Yellow Meadows friends, aside from an occasional email. But that's the thing about moving on, everyone does it. I guessed even if we stayed in Yellow Meadows, it wasn't guaranteed I would have kept the same friends forever. Plus, I loved New York, I truly did. I had adapted so easily, I met great people. I loved the big city, the theatre and even the blunt New Yorker's temperament.

However, it does bother me a bit that we won't be going back for Christmas. It almost feels like we're closing a chapter, even though I was just getting into the story. I was so lost in thought that I didn't even notice a knock on the door, until Mam's head came to view through the crack.

"We're ordering Chinese, are you in?"

I blinked. I was so sure she had come in to tell me about our Christmas plans, but maybe she'd chickened out.

"Sure," I replied automatically.

"Ok, cool. Is Will here?"

I looked around my bedroom but I couldn't see him, which is odd because he was always around, trying to sleep on my cushions. It did occur to me that Will was smart and knew how to hide well, so I curled myself to look under the bed. Mam had the same idea at the same time, lowering herself into a crouch.

I couldn't stop laughing when I found him there. Our fat white French bulldog, sleeping soundly under the bed on top of one of my pillows. A white, and once upon a time, clean pillow.

"What's wrong with this dog?" Mam wanted to know.

I looked at her from under the bed, with my head upside down. I watched as she shot me a gentle smile. Without thinking, I hopped back onto the bed to avert her gaze, "I don't know," I shrugged her question off.

That was Mam's second chance to tell me.

She didn't though, and I swallowed the annoyance inside of me. Okay... one more bone to throw at her; the biggest sign I was upset and maybe she should start a conversation, I avoided her eyes once more and started reading my book.

"Ok. I'll let you know when the food is here."

Mam closed the door and I kept staring at the book in front of me, even though the words made no sense. Like the most loyal friend I've ever had, Will came from under the bed with almost a limp after a great nap. I looked at his enormous kind eyes and I couldn't stop myself from smiling.

An inviting pet on the comfy bed, "Come here, Shakespeare."

CHAPTER TWO

"What?!"

Avery shrieked loudly whilst closing my locker with a loud snap, I frowned at her.

"This is amazing, it's literally the best news I've got all year," she said, ignoring the fact that because of her I had to put it in my locker's combination again.

"Are you listening to me? This works perfectly in our favour," Avery tried to close my locker once more so I'd look at her, but I held it open with a sigh, "Can I finish here?"

She smiled cheekily, letting me grab the book I wanted to bring home, and when I closed it finally on my own accord, Avery was already texting non-stop leaning on the other lockers beside mine.

Avery Nair, with the most perfect long black straight hair, caramel skin and quick wit was my best friend. We'd met on my first day at school. Immediately after I'd introduced myself to the class and sat down, I felt someone poke me with a pencil and on turning around, found Avery's puzzled expression.

"Why are you talking like that?"

I smiled a little, "Because… I'm Irish?"

She looked taken aback, and to my surprise, poked the boy in front of her, "Did you know that was an Irish accent?"

The boy turned. He had a cool hair cut, perfect high cheekbones, dark eyes and dark complexion. He looked at me and then Avery, "I guess, it was very lordy lordy lordy…"

I opened my mouth, trying to quickly make a decision on if they were indeed very rude or the funniest people I'd ever met.

"Maybe I should pick up an accent," Avery wondered aloud, while the boy laughed, "No, thanks, I don't want to go through the process of you choosing one." He looked at me with a bright white smile, "I'm Miles, this is Avery."

And that was that. Avery and Miles grew up together, living on the same street, they were the definition of the perfect friendship you only see on TV, but to my surprise they didn't even blink before including me into their little group, and five years later, here we were.

"Why would you skip Christmas in New York, anyway?" Avery wanted to know as I stepped away from my locker and headed to the exit.

"Because Christmas is the time to be with your family and loved ones?" I told her but I was half laughing even before I finished the sentence.

"Gross." That was Miles, coming from behind, with a nasty expression on his face. "What the hell are you guys talking about?"

"London is staying for Christmas."

Miles turned to me and nodded, "Cool."

"No!" Avery complained, "This is huge. She always misses the parties. It's literally the best time of the year."

Miles laughed a little and arranged his bag over the shoulder, "London is hardly the party queen."

"She would be if she stayed for the holidays," and turning, she grabbed my arm, "We have plans in place for all the social events over the next week."

We held the front of our coats as we stepped outside, and I buried my beanie hat further on my head to protect my ears. *"Avery* has plans for the social events" Miles corrected.

"Aren't you going?" I asked him, but it was Avery who replied, "Of course he will, Tania will be there."

Tania was Miles on and off and on again sort of girlfriend. They flirted constantly during school, but neither did anything about it. Parties though? They attracted each other like a moth to a flame.

"Maybe I'm done with Tania," Miles shrugged.

Avery scoffed, "Sure." And then facing me, "And think, all the stories we tell you in January, now you'll be able to experience them first-hand. Isn't that great?"

My "yes" was so weak I heard Miles stiff a laugh beside me. It was true, every year once I was back from Yellow Meadows, Avery and Miles came to my house for the whole weekend to fill me in on the ridiculous events that had happened in my absence. A little fire started to warm up in my chest as we made our way down to the subway.

Yes, so Miles was absolutely right, I wasn't exactly a party queen. But that didn't mean the social shenanigans of our school didn't intrigue me a little. Plus I might have my eye on someone…

"And Nathan will be there," Avery said, reading my mind.

I instantly felt my cheeks burn so red I'd be able to melt the ice.

Miles looked at me with a smile, "Stop, he likes you just fine."

"You don't really know that," I argued.

"Sure," he agreed over the noise of the train arriving. "But I kind of do," and winking at me, we stepped inside.

Miles always did this thing when I liked boys, he could tell from one look if they liked me back or not. I wasn't going to lie, Miles was so sure Nathan liked me back that I had to fight not to open a big gigantic silly smile right there.

"This is for the best, really," guaranteed Avery, but I was already on board.

Maybe I was born to be a party queen after all.

"We have a full calendar," Avery was saying, "Amanda is having a party on Friday, Lisa and Tina too."

"Aren't they best friends?" I asked confused, looking between the two.

"Yes," they replied simultaneously.

I shook my head with a small smile. Avery was now on her phone, suddenly acting like our little manager, telling us where we were going and when, explaining to me the half appearances we'd be making.

When I opened my mouth to spout about the unbelievable theatrics of some of these parties, Miles winked, "Every parent is extra generous because it's

Christmas."

"Especially this year. It's our last year all together." Avery said, as if I didn't know. Yes, it was our last year, soon we'll be going to college and I would have to part ways with one more group of friends. And while Miles, just like me, had plans to remain in New York, I knew Avery was applying to colleges in California. Let's be honest, she would do great there.

"I heard Bonnie Davis is hosting a pool party," Miles interrupted my thoughts.

"But it's December," I reasoned.

"Sure, but she's filthy rich and has a ginormous indoor pool," Avery interjected, eyes still glued to her phone.

"Isn't Bonnie the hippie girl that's always wearing upcycled rings as jewelry?"

"Yes?" Avery finally looked up, confused.

Miles snickered, "Being green is trendy, London."

"Sometimes her small-town self comes back to play," Miles said, shooting a look at Avery.

"It's cute," Avery smiled and I punched her boob.

"Stop," Avery caught my hand before I went for a second time, "Listen to me, be nice to mama Montgomery, you've got me? We have a full week ahead and I can't deal if you're grounded or something."

"When was I ever grounded?"

"Don't even start," Miles cut me off and raised an eyebrow.

"She still has to tell me we aren't going home,

you know?" I said with a small huff, crossing my arms over my chest.

"Well, when she tells you, be extra nice about it," he insisted, looking over our heads as we approached my stop.

I opened my mouth to complain. Were my friends telling me I wasn't always nice? But before I could get a word out, Avery reiterated, "No snarky comments. No prolonged silences with promises of revenge. Just be nice."

"It might sound like a wild concept..." Miles continued, "But just smile and say it's ok."

"Oh no, don't you think she's to get a little emotional? Be sad but understanding?"

Miles thought about it for a whole second and then nodded, "Ave is right. You got to milk it. Don't be crazy upset, but you know..."

"Enough for them to think going to the party is your second option."

"Going to the party *is* my second option," I reminded them.

"Parties," corrected Avery.

"You said..."

"Of course, because you won't be telling your beautiful mother that we are planning on three parties in one night."

Three parties. I barely knew most of the names Ave and Miles were dropping, and I bet none of those people knew mine.

"Of course they do," Miles rolled his eyes when I told them that.

"You live with Emmet Scott," laughed Avery.

I must have looked like a lost puppy, because

Miles felt inclined to say, "It's going to be fine. Lisa said it was just a get together."

Avery scoffed, "But you know what that means," turning to me she said, "Last year we partied for ten hours, and she hired a famous Australian DJ."

"If the party is so big why go to three of them?"

"They all live pretty close you know? We can make it on foot and see which one's the best."

I hummed. "It's starting to sound like a Gossip Girl episode and I am not a fan," I deadpanned.

Miles shook his head, "We're your friends, we hate people as much as you do, ok? But occasionally it is nice to let our hair down and play with the other humans."

"Plus there's loads of people you like there too. Like that one that is pretty good at science?"

"Lara?" I asked.

"Yes. She always goes, you like her right?"

I huffed, Lara was nice. Way nicer than any other names they dropped since.

We reached my stop and I busied myself going to the door. "I'll text when I talk to mam?" I called over my shoulder.

"She's gonna talk to her 'Mam'," Miles smiled to Avery.

I flipped them off, the door opened and I stepped out, still hearing Avery call after me, "The luck of the Irish to you."

.

CHAPTER THREE

Our home was suspiciously quiet. I knew Emmet was out since he was in rehearsal most of the afternoons, but Mam was off from her job for the Christmas break, and boy, oh boy, she loved Christmas. Ellis Montgomery was the loudest person during the holidays. She baked the nicest treats, she spoiled us with the most presents. She even attempted to sing, making the rest of us miserable. She was the Christmas Queen.

However, there was no sign of her. No cookies baking in the oven, no warbling voice, not even a sign of Will. I tried not to overthink, but now that I had plans, I wanted to get our talk over with.

That was my Mam for you. She'd overthink the smallest of things, come up with plans when most of the time I knew what was going on before she even had the time to tell me. Call it intuition, or maybe it was our strong mother-daughter bond. Whatever you like, I could read that woman like a book.

The stillness in the house was worrying, but I tried to ignore it. I padded my way to the kitchen, grabbing a bottle of water from the fridge. I dropped onto the nice dark blue velvet couch, which Will wasn't allowed on, and laughed when I saw it was full of white doggy hairs.

To my left the side our big fresh Christmas tree with beautiful coordinated colours looked over me. Every Christmas Mam chose our 'official' colours, which would be represented by the baubles and all the wrappings. This year our colours were blue and silver. Dark rich blue baubles and beautiful silver snowflakes, from the top to the bottom of our six feet tree. That's when the woman of the hour arrived, banging on the front door.

"Oh for fuck's sake off you go then."

"Mam?" I turned my head in her direction, but made no effort to move.

"Jesus, go! Get out of my sight. I'm done with you a lot."

Through the door came Will, racing and jumping on the couch beside me like it was no one's business. By instinct I reached out to scratch his ear when my mother came in, with a couple of shopping bags and a mad look on her face.

"What do you mean by 'you lot'."

"Your man found a couple of park friends." She said looking pointily at Will, who was trying to hide under me. "I thought it was going to be nice to bring him for a walk since I had to pick up a few things."

I turned to Will pouting, "Where are you being bold for mammy?"

"Don't you start, London," Mam's cross tone made me giggle again, and looking over at the shopping bags from the nicest stores in town, I arched an eyebrow, "What's the story with all of that?"

"It's Christmas. Had no one told you?"

"It felt odd when this old beardy man asked me to sit on his lap, but hey, it's New York."

Mam groaned, putting both her hands over her face, "Oh, don't even joke."

I gently kicked the bags laughing away, "Is it all for me?"

Of course I was fishing, I'm not that dumb. But it felt very on brand of my mother to decide to get something nice for me to soften the blow of the bad news she had to share.

"Maybe. Listen, I want to talk about Christmas."

"Great." I nodded, "Do you really think it's the season to be jolly?"

She rolled her eyes but I knew it wasn't for real, "What's up with Christmas?" I helped.

"I was thinking of maybe staying put this year." She shot.

"In New York?"

"It'll be fun. The three of us, nice presents...." Her eyebrows wiggled, "I can make turkey."

"I'm vegan."

"I can make vegan turkey."

"No, you can't."

"I can attempt making vegan turkey, give up and order from the nice vegan restaurant you like."

"That sounds more like it."

She laughed but seemed to be interested in what I was thinking. I let a breath out, scratching Will's ear again to have what to do with my hands.

"It's going to be weird not being in Yellow

Meadows for Christmas. What about Nana and Grandad?"

"Look…" Mam twisted her lips, "When was Nana ever happy with any of my decisions? But it will be grand, right? We can go next year."

I nodded slowly, knowing fully well it was killing my mother.

"Plus you can hang out with Avery and Miles!" She added, "They always call in after our holidays to tell you what's been happening. Now you can… you know, be part of it."

I frowned at her, trying my best not to smile, not to say a word.

"You mean going to the party?"

That took Mam for a second, but it was only for a single second and then, even though her voice wavered, she agreed, "Yes, sure, wouldn't that be fun?"

I shrugged and turned back to pet Will once more, "I guess."

Man stood up and clapped her hands together, "You'll see Daughter Dearest, it's going to be great. We'll have a gorgeous dinner in and you are going to have so much fun with your friends."

I did not let my smile creep in when I said, "Sure."

CHAPTER FOUR

Emmet wasn't that easily fooled. When Mam told him I was aware of our plans and I was to go to a party with Avery and Miles, my stepfather smiled over his cup of tea, "Isn't that sad? That instead of hanging out with your grandparents you have to stay here and go to a party with your friends?"

I shrugged, "I like Yellow Meadows."

Emmet hummed, "Aren't we lucky, Ellie?" He turned to Mam, "We have the only seventeen year old in the world that would prefer to play chess with her granddad than go to parties."

Mam did not detect the irony, she just smiled tenderly at me, so very proud of all the chess games I've ever played. I held my breath, but if Emmet was going to clue Mam in, he didn't do it in front of me. I gracefully excused myself before anything else was said.

Our Christmas plans were almost the same, even though we had this gigantic hole called Yellow Meadows in front of us. We shopped for presents for Nana and Grandad, and also my godfathers and

Mam's best friends Thad and Darren. Plus all the other people we loved the most. Mam got beautiful silver envelopes with glittery cards, and I wrote every single one of them using calligraphy.

I did not ask why she was taking so much care on wrapping the gifts when we both knew it would be in bits by the time it crossed the ocean. I did not ask why we weren't shopping online and delivering to them, instead of going through this whole post ordeal.

It was late that night and I was finishing the last silver bow on the top of Rina's signed copy of one of her favourite romance novels, when Mam sat on the couch behind me and took my hair on her hands to start a plait.

I waited.

She massaged my scalp and brushed back the baby hairs off my temple, "I know I agreed on letting you go out with Avery and Miles."

I said nothing, just waited some more.

"But… Would you tell me if something was wild, right?"

I laughed, "It's nothing wild, Mam. Have we met?"

"I know… I know. But… It's not like I don't want you to go…"

"It's just that you don't want me to go."

And I turned to her, letting the plait half done rest on my shoulder, "You've got to say the words, I don't like you tip-toeing around the subject."

I saw Mom biting her lip. "It's grand if you don't want me to go…"

"I never said that. But you know… Be careful. You'll stay with Avery and Miles, right?"

I turned again and she resumed the plait, "Yes, the party is just around the corner from Avery's. Is it ok if I sleepover?"

I could almost feel her stop breathing, but nothing came out but a strangled, "Sure."

Mam struggled with me growing up. I knew it and she knew it, but we didn't talk about it because tiptoeing around things was Mam's way. She liked to pretend to be this super cool young mother, which she was, so freaking out because a party might be off brand.

It was the whole single mother thing you know, for so long it was only Mam and I. We could tell each other's mood by just a look, it was us against the world. But suddenly we added Emmet to the mix, and then we moved countries and I grew and got a little more independent, and she struggled. And that was fine I guessed, but sometimes I would look at our lives and wonder where the Montgomery girls from Yellow Meadows went.

I found Will in my room, lazing on top of my bed, another piece of furniture he was not allowed on. I gathered the things I left, the mess which issued around my room after school. The next day was our last day of class before the Christmas break, and the three parties too. Avery asked about a million times if I was going, when I confirmed, saying yes and I was to sleep in her house she squeaked so loudly in my ear I wondered if I should stop answering her calls.

"And you told her you'll stay in my house for the weekend?" Avery wanted to know between classes.

"No, I'm not stupid."

We headed out to buy coffee in a nice little coffee shop just beside the school, we were going to wait for Miles, but we caught him beside the lockers having a very cosy chat with Tania.

"If I tell her right away she will know I'm planning something," I said while we waited on the line.

"That's true," Avery approved, and with a snap she closed her mouth.

That was very odd of Avery, she never missed an opportunity to talk. She was looking beyond me, so I followed her gaze, turning around to find Nathan had just arrived.

I closed my mouth with a snap too and I knew a stupid smile grew on me.

I knew three solid things about Nathan Miller:

1- He was good in sports, but I noticed him the first time because we were both in the same section of the library and we had a *moment*. He clearly enjoyed reading.

2- He moved here from Boston a year ago, and even though he was gorgeous I had not seen him parade around with a bunch of girls.

3- He had the most beautiful brown eyes I had ever seen.

I'm no expert, but those three things seemed to be enough to start a gigantic crush on him, which had evolved to an embarrassing level.

I watched as Nathan crossed the coffee shop, flicking his hazel hair and flashing those adorable dimples making all the girls swoon.

"Close your damn mouth," Avery snickered

behind me and I did as I was told.

"Hey, London," Nathan called to me when he was close enough.

"Hi, Nathan," I forced myself to sound normal.

He looked from one side to another, like he was thinking of something and when he turned back to me?

I melted.

Dead.

The end.

"So I was thinking," Nathan said, unaware that he had already killed me with one dimpled smile, "Are you going to Lisa's party?"

"Hmm, sure I was thinking about popping over."

Have I told you how cool I am?

I 'pop over' to cool house parties.

Nathan smiled easily, "Great, so I'll see you there?"

His hand brushed the hair out of his face while he talked to me and my heart fluttered in my chest.

Good god, how can someone be so charming? So... model like?

"Yeah, sure," Nonchalant London replied.

Nathan smiled, nodding and in a blink he was leaving me behind, my jelly legs unstable.

I felt Avery's sharp nails closing on my wrist and I knew she was holding in a scream. I turned quickly to control her, but her eyes were shining wildly.

"You were such a good actor," she said in a rushed whisper, "Even I believed you were that calm."

I laughed nervously, "Good. No one needs to

know how awkward I really am."

Avery smiled like I made her proud, and while grabbing my arm for dear life declared, "Tonight bring your skankiest dress."

CHAPTER FIVE

I looked myself up and down, and then once more. Avery was leaning over the desk in the corner of her massive bedroom, propped in front of the mirror finishing her makeup. Miles was laying on her very pink king size bed, eating Cheetos, with his shoes still on, even though Avery had asked him to remove them about four times.

"You look great, babes," Avery said.

I turned around and bit my lip. I'd been looking at myself in the full length mirror since I'd arrived in my velvet black dress, black boots and a white turtleneck. My wavy brown hair was in a half ponytail and I'd do minimal makeup.

Hmmm.

"You look great," Miles said from the bed, "Very you."

I turned around to face the mirror once more, now with a frown forming. I didn't want to look like myself, whatever the hell that meant.

I wanted to be the party queen, and while Avery did not complain when I rang her bell an hour ago, this was definitely not the skankiest dress I owned.

"He likes you because you are wholesome little London Montgomery."

Miles tsked with his mouth full of Cheetos, "The way you're saying it sounds bad. Lon, don't mind Avery, you look great."

"Thanks," I said, distracted by my own reflection.

"I think her wholesome self is wonderful, thank you very much," Avery was saying in the background, and without warning I felt her arms embrace me from behind and her head rested on my shoulder while we looked at our reflection in the mirror.

Avery blew me a kiss with her blood red lips, "Don't you ever be insecure. I will slap the bitches who don't appreciate my London."

I made a face but nodded at the same time, my friend smiled brightly and let me go, and we both turned to Miles, who was still eating Cheetos on the bed.

"For fuck sake Miles Carter, stop fucking with my bedspread!"

The music was loud in party number one. Lisa McDonald was someone I'd never exchanged two words in the five years we'd known each other, but I knew plenty about her.

I knew she was rich as were most people from our school, I knew she was very interested in music since her Dad was a music producer and they knew all New York City bands.

And that was why when I arrived in her back

garden my jaw dropped. Lisa transformed a garden into a nightclub. Obviously shocked, I squeezed Avery's hand while she was bringing us among the crowd.

Avery laughed, "I know, babes."

In front of us was a fully equipped stage, lights and even a smoke machine. A tall marquee protected everyone from the rain or snow, while electric heaters kept us warm. I was officially in awe.

We finally reached the right side where there was a fully functioning bar and Miles called us, "Vodka and lime?" We both nodded, and Miles called the barman over everyone's head. Soon we had our drinks in hand and Avery shoved us to the side where it was less crowded.

"This is insane," I tasted my drink, "Aren't they scared of the police shutting this down?"

Avery laughed and shook her head, "No cops will shut down a Lisa McDonald party, London. Relax."

I was feeling a little better when I finished my first drink and the band started their set. Avery and I danced together, making up funny dance moves rather than actually trying to be cool while Miles laughed with us. He got us a second drink which we drank happily and when I was feeling that warm alcoholic fuzzy feeling I saw Nathan, just across from us, with a beer, beside the house's back door.

"Go!" Avery said to my ear and off I went.

I knew I had rosy cheeks from all the dancing and the vodka but I was hoping it was endearing rather than making me look like a drunk mess. I snuggled into my faux leather jacket and marched into Nathan's direction. His bright smile was the first thing I saw, and then those damn dimples.

"London," He said in an easy going manner, and to my surprise, came closer, giving me a half hug.

I breathed in his delicious smell and felt even drunker than before.

"Hey, Nathan,"

"It's packed. I didn't think I was going to find you."

I looked up to him with a shy smile, "Here I am."

"Do you want a drink?"

"Yeah… I would love a can of coke."

Nathan winked at me and turned on his heels to fetch me a can, I used the time to fix my clothes and gather my wits.

I was going to kiss Nathan Miller, that was a fact. He was clearly interested and I was more than willing.

Breathe in and out.

Ok, so it was happening, which was great, I just needed to be ready for it.

It wasn't a big deal really, since I broke up with my first boyfriend, Luke, I've been on dates and occasionally kiss a boy, but I've never built up a crush this big. I had never idolized someone so much, and god knew it was very dangerous territory.

Nathan was back with my can and I awkwardly drank it. The band was playing again, even louder than before, and with a torturous gorgeous smile, Nathan whispered into my ear:

"You want to dance?"

I nodded, he took my hand and he parted the

crowd. Just like Avery did before, Nathan guided me right into the middle of the dance floor by the hand. I heard a few people from our school waving at us, and I heard a few "Hey, Miller!", which Nathan answered easily, and just as I thought we were never going to stop, we did and he turned to me.

The music wasn't very sexy or romantic, it was a catchy indie rhythm that did enough to get us out of our feet and bobbing our heads up and down. Nathan did not let my hand go once while we danced non-stop I found myself laughing and finally being goofy with him.

He seemed to be enjoying himself, enjoying my company and I felt stupid for being so insecure before.

When the music finished and the band announced a short break, Nathan's hands came to my elbow and I felt goosebumps up the back of my neck.

"I'm so happy you're here with me," he told me, and while it felt odd since we had not come together, I was pleased he was being open.

"Me too," I let myself be honest.

"You're amazing, do you know that?"

I shrugged and looked down to my shoes and my cheeks were back to bright red, I heard Nathan chuckle, "God, you're so cute."

I was shaking my head, when he came forward and embraced me in a hug, kissing the top of my head, "I'm just going to get us drinks, ok? Will you wait here?"

I nodded and he smiled once more before stepping away and getting lost in the crowd.

That was going great, wasn't it? I looked all around trying to see if I could find Miles and Avery but I was hardly seeing into distance. Even on my tiptoes I couldn't find Miles' head in the crowd and I wondered if he was with Tania already.

It was fine, we'd see each other eventually, I was sure Avery wasn't going to be shy about dragging me around for the next party when it was time.

I bobbed my head to the song playing on the speakers, it was way lower than when the band was on the stage which allowed people to start talking around me.

I started to feel like he was taking too long, but soon I had my answer of why there was a delay. I looked up and my mouth fell open to the sight in front of me.

He was on the stage.

On the stage?

Why was Nathan on the stage?

I frowned slightly and went up my tiptoes again, trying to see if it was an illusion, but when someone screamed, "Yeah, Miller!" I knew it must be Nathan up there.

He had an acoustic guitar strapped on him, I stepped back without even realising what I was doing and bumped into a chest, turning my head not even seeing who it was. I said distractedly, "I'm sorry."

"No problem," The stranger replied, but my eyes were already back on the stage.

Why the hell was he up there?

"Hey, everyone," Nathan said into the mic and a bunch of people woohooed him, I didn't.

"I hope you don't mind me taking the mic for a second while the band takes a break."

People cheered and I imagined they didn't

mind. Jesus, why didn't he say he was going to sing or whatever? Why tell me he was going to get us drinks and leave me there waiting in the middle of a bunch of randomers?

Was it a split second decision maybe?

No way, who the hell is on their way to the bar when all of the sudden they decide to go onto the stage?

And did he have that guitar before? Is he one of those guys who strolls into parties with a silly guitar on hand waiting to play something for the group?

Oh man…

His hands found the strings making a slow melody while he talked to all of us, "I just had to say something. I'm here with this amazing girl… She's just incredible, you know the type of girl that you want to be around all the time?"

I involuntarily stepped back again, bumping once more to the person behind me, "I'm sorry," I said absentmindedly and the same deep voice replied, with a chuckle: "No problem."

"You know when you meet someone and it all clicks?"

The crowd was going insane, every girl around was melting one by one by his words, and my stomach dropped when I started to recognise the strum of melody he was playing.

Shit.

Shit.

"This is for you London Montgomery!"

Many things happened at the same time; Everyone around turned to look at me with very different expressions, ranging from knowing smiles to indifference and jealousy, I turned bright red of course.

Then, stepping back once more I bumped into the same person for the third time and while my mouth wanted to say sorry one more time, my brain couldn't make the words as Nathan started to sing "More than Words".

I felt a warm hand coming to mine, and the deep voice behind me whispered, "Let's get out of here."

And we did.

CHAPTER SIX

"What kind of maniac, bat shit crazy person does something like that?"

I shrieked as soon as Lisa McDonald's gate closed behind us, "And 'More Than Words'? Is there a tackier song?"

"No, I don't think so," my new companion murmured.

"And on our first date? I mean that wasn't even a date since we came separately. Why... why would someone go up on a stage to sing the worst song ever to a person he hadn't even kissed?"

"Was that the first interaction you had? Right there on the dance floor?"

"Virtually yes! I mean, I see him everyday at school but we never sit down to talk. Of course, because if he had talked to me, he would know singing that shit song in front of the whole school is literally what my nightmares are made of!"

I stopped myself in the middle of the road.t felt like I had run out of steam, I turned to my right for the first time to look properly at the person I was walking with.

Tall, short buzz cut and a little curve on his full lips. Dark brown skin and under the streetlights his eyes were almost yellow, even though I knew they must be green or hazel, or a mix of both.

"I'm London by the way," I said.

"I've heard," he replied and I couldn't miss the humour in his voice.

My eyes widened when I remember that not only Nathan sang the terrible song and said those things, but he also announced my name to everyone. My companion laughed of my panic, "I'm Augusto."

"Hi, Augusto, welcome to my personal hell."

We walked for a second, my hands buried in my face, and then I snapped out of it, where the hell was I going?

On instinct I reached to my right pocket for my phone and panic ensued when I realised there was nothing there.

"Fuck…"

Augusto stopped beside me, "What's wrong?"

"Fuck…" I said once more checking the other pocket in a frenzy, and then pretty much patting myself up and down like my phone decided to travel from my pocket to my ass.

"My phone," I cried, "I don't have my phone."

"It's ok," August said in such a calming tone I wondered if it was really ok, "You can use mine."

I looked at his extended hand offering me the phone and I sighed sadly, "I don't know anyone's number but my mother's. And I am not calling her."

"We can go back to the party…" He said but the thought of going back to the room with Nathan and his silly song made my skin crawl.

I shook my head, "It's ok. I know there's two more parties around here and my friends are going there after Lisa's. I'm sure someone from school will let me borrow their phone to ring them. It's fine."

Augusto nodded and we kept walking, making me turn to him, "Where are *you* going?"

"With you." He said, shrugging.

"Excuse me?"

"It's late and you don't have your phone, it's not safe. At least I can call the police if we need to."

I scoffed, "I don't know you. I mean, are you a robber or a rapist?"

"Nope."

"That's what a criminal would say."

I looked to my side and I caught when his lips curved in a smile, "When we get to the party you can get rid of me."

"Ok, go on then."

We walked in silence, the only sound was our steps and the far away traffic, I was praying under my breath, because while I knew the general direction of Tina's party, I did not have the exact address.

"You really aren't that guy's girlfriend?" He broke the silence making me turn with a gigantic frown.

"Of course not! He didn't ask me out!"

Augusto chuckled, raising his arms up, "Hey, I'm just checking. I would help you to escape anyway."

"Well, thanks. But no, he's insane. And right now probably the whole school thinks we're dating," I looked at him for a second and shook my head, "The audacity... Just boils my blood."

I noticed that he nodded, but I shut my trap

right away. I didn't know him. Why the hell had I followed him out and agreed to bring him to the party? It was beyond me and my better judgment.

"Hmm, do you know Lisa?"

"No," He said, "My brother knows a guy from the band, I had nothing better to do so…" He shrugged like it was enough of an explanation.

It wasn't.

"Alright… So you don't go to my school?"

"No."

"How old are you?"

He turned to me smiling, "Seventeen."

Ok, so at least he was school-age and not some creepy old dude with a baby face.

"I'm on holidays with my family," He offered, "From Sao Paulo."

"As in…"

"São Paulo, Brasil."

"I know where Sao Paulo is," I huffed.

"You looked confused for a second there."

"Well, I wasn't."

"Me, my parents and my brothers are on our way to spend Christmas with my sister, she lives in Europe. Mom decided to spend a few days here before our connecting flight."

"I see…" I nodded, looking ahead.

"I didn't know anyone in the party until you started bumping into me," he smirked, way too charismatically.

I twisted my lips, "Well, sorry about that. I was a little taken aback at the time, you see."

"I know. Some dude was declaring his undying love to you."

I groaned, "Stop reminding me!"

He thought that was funny, "It happened ten minutes ago, I don't need to remind you of anything."

I refrained from answering, as we turned right onto what I was almost sure was Tina's street. I expected to hear the same commotion as from Lisa's house, but the street was silent. I cursed under my breath.

"Are you sure it's here?"

"No," I shook my head. Maybe I did need to call my mother. She sure would be furious, but I hoped she could understand why I needed to leave that party in such a hurry.

With no phone…And a stranger.

It was very unlikely that Mam would forgive that part. Cringe when I tell her about Nathan? Sure. But she wouldn't think it is cute of me fleeing in such a hurry just because of embarrassment.

I was weighing in my options when Augusto said, "What the hell is that?"

I looked up and saw it, right in front of a beautiful house with pristine windows, in the middle of the lawn stood the six guards. Three each side of the door.

Uniform, monkey masks and wings.

Flying monkeys.

"Oh, for fuck sake… Let's go," I huffed and Augusto followed me to the entrance.

CHAPTER SEVEN

I pushed open the door like I was invited. If Augusto thought it was rude, he didn't dare to utter a word.

It was yet another ridiculous example of ostentation coming from the people I saw every single day at school. People I never thought much of, people like Tina who looked perfectly normal but now I knew were completely insane judging by her choice of party.

As crazy as Lisa's party was, at least it felt like a normal party any teenager would be glad to attend. But Tina's?

From the flying monkey's outside, the perfectly laid yellow bricks coming from the front door to up the stairs, to the clearly hired actors walking around dressed as lion, tin man and scarecrow, Tina's party was a theatre kid's wet dream. Everyone else would think it was bananas.

I had no words. Why the hell all of that?

A sigh from me, the rare times I got long emails from my friends back home they always talked about who kissed who behind the green, who was drunk at the field, who cut the skirt too short just to upset their teachers. Silly rebellions, silly micro things that made us all feel powerful.

New York kids though? I mean, at least the ones I knew… It was like the sky was the limit and of course, the budget was endless.

And even though I went to the same school as them, had a famous stepfather and a Mam with a really fancy job nowadays, still I could picture their faces if I ever suggested something of this magnitude.

"These people go to school with you?" I felt Augusto's breath on my right ear, when the Scarecrow passed us.

"These thirty years old? Nope."

He chuckled, "No, I meant her," And he pointed to the left of us, where in a bigger room, under a chandelier where staff carried trays with something I bet was champagne, in the middle of it all was Tina looking like the mirror image of Judy Garland.

"Oh yes…"

Augusto laughed beside me again, "Your school is weird."

Weird or not, Tina and the people she was surrounded by were the only hope to contact Miles or Avery and with that hopeful thought I marched through the crowd and only stopped when our favourite Judy wannabe was in front of me.

Her famous sugary smile opened up, "London! You're here!"

We weren't friends, but we weren't enemies. I had no reason to dislike Tina, she was nice and overly sweet to anyone who crossed her path. Yes, I had no patience for her theatrics, sure. Did she organise too many school plays and events? Yes. But Tina worked hard in whatever she decided to do, and if nothing, that was a damn amazing quality.

"Yeah, surprise," And I swear I meant it in a friendly way, but by the scoff I heard from Augusto, who was still trailing after me, I knew it sounded more sarcastic.

"You're never here this time of year, sweetie," Tina batted her long eyelashes at me and grabbed a glass from a passing waiter.

"Would you like a drink?"

"Thanks…" I shook my head.

"Oh, but I insist,"

I opened and closed my mouth like a fish, and it was the person beside me who took the situation on his own hands.

Augusto was just stepping away from me, but he reached for the champagne with no problem, and I heard the "Thank You" coming from him.

Like it was the first time Tina had ever seen a boy, her eyes sparkled in interest and she smiled up to him, "Now who are you?"

"I'm Augusto, sorry for intruding in your party."

"What a great name!" She gushed, and I turned slowly to catch right on time when Augusto winked at her. I couldn't stop myself, I went right in and rolled my eyes.

"Tina, do you have Avery's number?"

She turned to me, much less interested now Augusto was in the game, and blinked slowly.

"I don't think so," and all of the sudden back and forth between us, "I thought you were dating

Nathan."

Jesus almighty! Sorry, I'm Irish catholic, my curses tend to get very religious.

"We got separated and I don't know where my phone is…"

"Do I hear an accent? Where are you from, Augusto?"

My mouth fell open. Was I invisible? Was I completely utterly see-through? I turned my head to watch my companion smile slowly at the host, like it wasn't the rudest thing that had ever happened.

"Brazil," And I bet my favourite boots he rolled that R more than necessary.

Tina gasped, bringing her hand to her chest, "Oh that's just absolutely gorgeous!"

Was she… putting on an accent too? You have to love Tina. She had everything, the looks, the talent, the determination- and judging by the size of her house, she had literally everything. So why not practice a made up accent that only old Hollywood stars use?

Tina said one thing or another about visiting Rio de Janeiro with her family last year, the Mid-Atlantic accent dripping off every fake word and I wondered who the hell she thought she was fooling. Her Dad was from Milwaukee.

Augusto smiled through her anecdote and told her he had no idea what she was talking about because he was indeed from Sao Paulo.

"You've got to admire Brazilians," Tina was telling us, "Such a marvellous sense of the most important things in life, which are of course a nice tan and a cocktail."

She laughed loudly and I winced. Did that

sound terrible or was I just annoyed they were ignoring me?

My questions were answered when I saw the discomfort flash across Augusto's face for a second and but like an expert on masking real feelings, the charming smile was back in place and the silky voice was saying, "I couldn't tell you. Sao Paulo is one of the biggest metropolitan cities in the world, we are far too used to going up our gigantic skyscrapers and making money. But I understand the gringo fantasy, it's vaguely amusing. Not very clever, though."

The last sentence he said copying the ridiculous way she was talking, over enunciating the hell of the 'vaguely amusing'. I almost swallowed my tongue.

Tina had the decency to turn a very distinct shade of red, "I didn't mean to…" completely dropping the accent.

Augusto shook his head, raising a hand, "Don't worry, I'm not easily offended."

She opened her mouth again, but I really suspected she had nothing better to say, nothing that would make an impact. Tina started so well with the flirting, I mean, before the accent and the stereotype… Well, maybe she should work on her flirting.

"Tina," I sighed, interrupting the awkward silence, "Do you know anyone that can help me with Avery or Miles' number?"

She looked back at me almost wincing in an apology for the horrible way she dealt with the situation, "I saw Tania around."

I could punch her for making me wait all that time for that simple information, I grunted a very ungraceful thank you and turned around.

CHAPTER EIGHT

"Are you upset?"

I looked around the main party hall, everything was perfectly Wizard of Oz themed and it did look beautiful. I tried to avoid looking at Augusto, but when he didn't answer straight away, I had no option but to turn to him.

His hazel eyes shone under the light and he gave me that slow smirk, "Nah."

"She was rude," I confirmed.

"Yes, she was. But that's to show how rich and uneducated you can be."

I frowned, even though I was holding a smile, "You're very chill."

Almost to prove me right he rolled his shoulders relaxed, and I let out a little tiny giggle, "My sister always says: What people think about you is their problem not yours."

"Your sister is smart," I told him, looking around again for any sign of Tania, "Is she the one you're visiting for Christmas?"

"Yes. She's my oldest and only sister, and I have two older brothers."

"That's a lot. So you're the youngest?"

"Yes."

"Hmm."

"What about you?"

I turned back to him and he was having a sip of his drink completely relaxed in the mix of people he didn't know. Wasn't that amazing? I went to school with the same faces for five years and still my nerves sky rocketed before the party, yet here was Augusto. Completely at home, not a bother in the world, even though he knew no one and was not just out of his comfort zone but out of his time zone.

Maybe I should learn a thing or two from him.

"I'm an only child," I shared, "Where's she?"

From right to left I couldn't see where Tania could possibly be, I lapped the room twice and still nothing. In the back of my mind the worries were rushing back, I had transportation, no phone and no one I trusted with me.

Augusto got a few extra points for the last minutes but he was still a virtual stranger. And the fact my only hope was someone who didn't even like me did not escape me either.

"I saw her with Miles in the other party," I sighed more to myself than Augusto, "But I lost them in the crowd so she could have left..."

"Or maybe Tina was mistaken?"

I scoffed, "Wouldn't be the first time."

We shared a little smile and Augusto dropped into action, "Ok, let's go separate ways to cover the whole party and we'll meet back here in ten minutes."

I nodded but my belly thumbed a little. While I was being very practical about the whole ordeal the situation did make me a little scared, I knew him for only an hour but the idea of getting separated from him also terrified me.

Augusto's eyes watched me carefully for a second, and like he was reading my mind, offered me a little smile, "Don't worry. I will be back here in this exact spot in ten minutes."

I wanted to deny it, but I wasn't that full of bullshit, Augusto wouldn't let me be anyway, interrupting he said; "Just describe her to me so I have an idea of who I'm looking for."

You know what's not fair? Asking you to describe someone you don't like fairly.

I couldn't just say the obvious things; she looked like Demi Lovato, because I had to add that the personality wasn't a match, even though she had a big "Sorry not Sorry" energy.

Tania was a difficult character, one because she was in a yoyo relationship with my best friend, and every time they were on the other side of the yo-yo she had no qualms in bad mouthing him to the entire school. She would talk out of her ass for a whole week but kiss him on Saturday night and while I knew it was their thing and had nothing to do with me, I still wasn't much impressed.

On the other hand, well, she didn't like me either. Avery and Miles were childhood best friends so people at school got used to them coming together, but I was the new girl and to Tania I obviously had something for Miles.

Which maybe... just maybe, hear me out... I never really denied.

Listen, Avery knew I didn't like Miles like that,

Miles knew it and I knew it too but that uncertainty wrecked Tania's brain so I let her run with it.

I didn't hug him more than normal, I didn't flirt with him just because, but I never went out of my way to make her feel safer and I guessed that was on me.

Especially now when I needed her.

"She's pretty. Like super pretty," I swallowed, "Dark brown shoulder length hair, and she really looks like Demi Lovato."

"Ok, Demi Lovato, I can work with that."

He moved quickly away from me and I almost thought of asking him to stay, but I didn't because that was silly as hell.

I needed to find Tania and call my friends, I needed to get my ass back with them and say thank you to my eager companion but *let him go*.

I passed the usual people who I knew would adore this kind of drama filled atmosphere. The other theatre kids, who considered Tina truly their Judy Garland, and even the ones who did not like her.

The golf club kids were here too, not that they actually played golf, but that was the nickname Avery and I gave to them. We believed they were so unbelievably posh, they probably golfed the whole afternoon after school.

Plus they never seemed to be really involved in anything, they just pranced around school, barely interested in what was going on.

I turned right after the main hall and started to doubt that Tania was really there, but right during that thought I heard the boisterous laugh coming from the end of the hall and a very loud exclamation in Spanish.

Tania.

I almost ran down the hall and when I reached the end I found Tania and her friends laughing in the bathroom, Tania and another one over the sink retouching their makeup in the mirror, while the rest were on the other side telling a story in very fast Spanish.

They stopped and looked at me all at once.

"Tania you're here!" the words escaped out of me without forethought as to what sounds cool.

"Who's this?" Someone snickered at the back, they all knew who I was and I guessed that was the joke.

I gulped, "I lost my phone back in Lisa's party and I have no way to contact... Avery."

Shit, that's how scared I was. No balls to ask for Miles' number. But Tania was smart, she looked me up and down with her perfect eyebrow raised, "I don't have Avery's number."

She said like it was a challenge, she was daring me to come over and ask for Miles' number, and that was exactly what I had to do.

"They're my ride home," I told her, trying to get around saying Miles' name.

No reaction. Absolutely none, they just kept looking at me like no words had just left my lips. I opened my mouth and closed it again, wondering what could be said to make Tania and her minions to acknowledge me.

"Oh, you found her."

Saving me one more time, here comes Augusto.

CHAPTER NINE

Tania's first sign that she was actually a human was to slowly switch her gaze from me to Augusto, from disdain to mildly interested.

I took the opportunity, "As I was saying, they're my ride and I lost my phone."

Augusto then fished his phone from his front pocket and unlocked it while looking at Tania, "Just call out the number."

He said it in a way when you know something isn't a problem, like when you ask someone for directions to the bathroom. I had to appreciate his approach, it was so sincere and unassuming that I almost took a second to comprehend it actually worked. Tania called out the number digit by digit, hating me a little every step of the way.

Augusto handed me the phone, "It's ringing."

Tania probably had the opportunity to hate me more because I simply turned on my heels with the phone plastered to one ear and a finger to the other. As the phone rang and rang I prayed for a miracle, it never occurred to me that if Miles was in a party he wouldn't notice his phone ringing.

"Hello?"

A relieved breath escaped me, "Miles!"

"Who's this?"

I rolled my eyes, "It's London, you clown. Where are you guys at?"

"Amanda's. You disappeared, Avery looked everywhere and…"

"Ok listen, just stay where you are and I will meet you."

"Ok. Not moving," he mocked.

"Don't mess with me right now."

"Come over," He laughed and ratted off the address.

I felt lighter knowing it wasn't very far from Tina's.

I turned to look for Augusto, but he was following closely once more. I bumped straight into him, his chest to mine, my hand holding his phone between us. When I looked up and there he was… Smiling down to me. That big slow grin that had appeared many times in the last couple of hours we spent together, the little glint into his hazel eyes.

I gulped and stepped back.

"Thank you," I said looking at the phone still between us.

"No problem," not making a move to grab the phone from me.

"I'm meeting Miles now. Er.., thank you for your help tonight."

"That's all good."

I felt suddenly very awkward, like I just realised how weird the time we spent together was. He was a stranger, the kind and helpful kind, but still a stranger nevertheless.

I stepped away once more, "Hope you have a good night."

"You too," he called from the same spot, definitely not feeling any awkwardness whatsoever.

I felt compelled to add something more but it fell flat on my tongue, so I nodded and he smiled again and then I turned and left.

The only noise at the street was the clicking of my boots, I held my jacket close to my body and shook off the effect Augusto's calm had on me.

It was funny how some people are just so confident and certain of themselves that they can sashay through life without really worrying what everyone thinks of them. I was with him for about two hours and I could tell he was one of those silent confident types.

At Amanda's address I found nothing out of the ordinary. I mean, it looked like a regular house for this neighbourhood and if it wasn't for the few gangs of teenagers hanging out the front lawn I wouldn't suspect there was a party there.

But then I stopped.

Why was everyone in their pyjamas?

I turned left to right and every single person was wearing nightwear, and yes I'm not such a buzzkill to be hating on a classic pyjama party, but after the night's shenanigans the idea of seeing my classmates in their house clothes was nothing short of terrifying.

I was tired, it felt like a long ass night, whatever vodka and lime I had at Lisa's party it was already long gone from my system.

I entered Amanda's house, the third party of

the night and even my tiredness wasn't enough to hold my surprise at the decoration.

Like a gigantic room, pillows, cushions everywhere, feathers hanging from the ceiling like they were falling on us and every single person was appropriately dressed but me. I walked around for a second a little stunned once more by the amount of effort these girls put into their parties, especially when they were all having them on the same night.

"Ah, good, you're here!"

I turned to find Miles and Avery coming to me, *in their pyjamas*. Miles had a white t-shirt and boxers on and Avery was in the nicest silkiest little sleeping dress with a lacy hem, in the most mesmerizing lavender.

"Why are you both dressed like that?" I gasped.

"It's a pyjama party, Lon," Avery said like I was a bit thick.

I shook my head, did they bring a change of clothes with them? Why the hell had they never told me? I was going to ask about a million questions, but Avery grabbed my arm and pulled me away from the hall to a smaller room on the right side.

"What happened between you and Nathan?" Avery whispered his name, trying not to alert the other people what we were talking about.

I sighed in the most annoyed way, "I think he's insane! Did you hear what he said…?"

Miles nodded with a gigantic smile on him while Avery giggled, "More than words?" More laughs.

"It's the tackiest song in the world," I cried, "We never went out, we didn't even kiss! How is your first reaction after an interaction to go ahead and sing about it?"

"Maybe he was already in love with you..." Avery wondered, with a clear laugh in her voice.

"Yes, he loved me in secret so damn much that he had to bust into song," I shook my head, "Can we go?"

"Oh no! You can't go right now!" Avery held my hands into hers and looked at Miles for help.

"Lon," my other friend said, "if I get you a drink and you sit and relax a bit? Nathan isn't here, fuck that creep. What do you think?"

I bit my lip. I really did want to have a nice relaxing time with my friends, and while half of the night had been a disaster, still we could turn this around, right?

I nodded to Miles who was more than ready to go fetch me a drink, and Avery dragged me to another room where the music was louder and the lighting lower. She grabbed my hips to sway them for me and I let myself laugh, Miles handed me a drink and I took straight away.

It was fine, the night wasn't over yet and with one more drink I could certainly forget the whole "More than words" issue.

We danced for almost an hour, I had to ditch my turtle neck and tie my jacket over my waist because I was so damn hot.

"We need to order pizza after this..." I said into Avery's ear.

"YES!" She jumped up and down and passed the message to Miles who agreed right away.

I shook my head with a silly smile on my face and excused myself to find the bathroom, my friends did not care, they simply waved me away and kept dancing in the most silly way imaginable.

I found a bottle of water on my way to the bathroom and gladly finished half of it in one gulp. The line for the bathroom was big enough to annoy me a little, but not as big to make me change my mind. I leaned on the right wall as a couple of girls I knew from the year younger than me, started gossiping about everyone in the party.

I half listened to them while waiting, drinking a strategic sip of water every time I felt like laughing.

That was when I heard, just by my left ear the slow dragged words, nice accent and low timbre:

"I have a theory, do you want to hear it?"

CHAPTER TEN

I swallowed all wrong and half of the bottle ended up down my top, followed by the most inhumane noise escaping me as I turned and found Augusto smiling down at me.

"Are you stalking me?" I asked, trying to dry my dress.

He laughed, "No. Do you want to hear my theory?"

"The only reason why you would be here is if you followed me around. That's creepy as shit."

He shook his head, "I called a friend after you left and they asked me to meet them here."

My eyes narrowed in suspicion, but he kept the smile on his face, "I can introduce you to him, if you like."

"I think that will be necessary."

Augusto's eyebrows raised, "I thought we were becoming friends…"

"That was before you followed me here."

He shook his head in that way people do when they are amused, I open my mouth to say something but he interrupted me;

"Go ahead, it's your turn."

I turned around and he was right, the chatty girls were gone and the bathroom door was left open. I stepped inside and the last thing I saw was Augusto's amused face before I locked the door.

When I left the bathroom he wasn't there anymore.

Hmm.

I looked side to side, and I couldn't find him. I moved back to the dance floor and Avery and Miles were still there right where I left them, but Augusto wasn't anywhere to be seen.

Maybe he was a hallucination..

And I truly would believe that if I haven't used his phone.

His phone!

I reached my friends and went on my tiptoes to ask Miles for his phone. You've gotta give to him, he didn't even bat an eyelid to my request, just gave it to me and kept dancing and goofing around with Avery.

I opened the recent calls and shot a message to that number;

"Is it your game to just freak me out and disappear?"
"Nope."

I bit my lip and frowned and that's when he sent me another one: *"I just came back to my friends, I didn't need to go to the toilet."*

"Where are you?"

I thought he was going to play hide and seek and not say anything since took him a minute to reply, but eventually I got:

"On the left hand side of the hall. It's an office."

And, god knows why, I told my friends I was

stepping out of dancing for a second, giving the phone back to Miles. They agreed but told me not to leave without them.

There was something to be said about the willingness in me to go to him. In very clear London Montgomery fashion I didn't want to think about it.

When I came through the door, I was relieved to find the first sign this was a normal party after all: a bunch of guys playing beer pong.

Augusto was to one side at the table with two other guys playing against the other three.

"So you actually know people?"

He turned to face me and his face broke into a smile, I held my own.

"I'm not a liar," he said easily, "That's my brother Dante," Augusto pointed to the older and slightest shorter version of himself across the table.

And before I could add that having his brother meant nothing in the whole stalking scheme of things, he continued, "And that's his boyfriend Carlos who is friends with Amanda's older brother, Ash."

Carlos was in the other team with Dante, but my face went scarlet when I noticed indeed, just beside Augusto, was Ashton Wilder, Amanda's brother. He was a couple of years older than us, but I saw him around the school before he graduated.

Ok, so he proved he wasn't a stalker, that was great for me right? No one really wants a stalker.

"Can you play?" Ashton asked me and I found myself nodding.

I wasn't a beer pong genius, but come on, it was an easy concept. Ashton and the other guy in Augusto's team opened space for me and Augusto held the little ball between his fingers with a smile on his face.

I took the ball and positioned myself right in the middle. As I said, I wasn't a beer pong expert so it wasn't a surprise when the ball didn't even pretend to fall correctly in a cup.

They laughed in an easy going way like it wasn't a big deal, but when Dante threw it went straight away in the cup right in front of me and I got a little splash.

The third guy in "our" team took the cup, removing the little ball and giving it to me, "Have another try," he said drinking the beer.

I positioned myself again when I heard Augusto, "Do you need help?"

"It's one of those 'teaching the girl something' scenes?"

He chuckled and to my surprise kept up with my joke with no hesitation, "I do think standing behind you would be great, but something tells me you're not very into gender stereotypes."

I whipped my head to him, was he flirting with me? Was he flirting with me with feminism? Because that might work.

I shook my head and faced ahead, "So how would you help me?"

"Bend your knees, back straight and hold your breath."

"Is that a real technique?"

He shrugged, "Works in many different sporty scenarios. You might as well try."

I did what I was told, and really tried my best, but of course that wasn't going to be the moment I realised I was actually a prodigy. Augusto laughed and his friends too, Ashton came over to take my position saying, "While we still have a chance," and I let him because, let's be honest, I wasn't getting good anytime soon.

I went to the side and Augusto was with me, we watched a couple of points and it wasn't hard to see the other team had clearly an advantage.

"Where are your friends?" Augusto asked.

"Back there dancing," I turned to face him, "They made me promise I wasn't going to leave them behind this time."

"When you need to run, you need to run," He said again in that very easy going way and now that I wasn't so worried about my current situation I started to appreciate that maybe Augusto was flirting with me all along.

"I need air, this house is so warm," I tried to distract myself, not really moving exactly, but shifting my gaze away from him.

"Come over here," He grabbed me by the hand through the double glass door at the office to the side garden.

I went out and instantly felt better, I knew I was being an idiot for going out with no jacket in December when I was all sweaty, for sure that was something Mam would yell about, but just add that to the list.

"How old is your brother?" I asked for no other reason but to make small talk.

"Nineteen. He was living in New York for his gap year, that's how he met Carlos. They are doing the long distance thing since."

"And then you have another older brother and

then your sister?"

"Yep. Marcela and Mariano are twins, they are twenty-seven."

I nodded and suddenly felt a cold breeze up my spine, I untied the jacket and put it back on, "Your parents must be real chill... I mean you guys are in another country and partying with strangers. Mam wasn't keen on letting me come and I see these losers everyday."

Augusto shrugged, "Mom and Dad are... eccentric, can I say that?"

"You can say whatever."

"They travel most of the year, they hopped all over. Mainly based in Barcelona for the last...?" A little laugh, "I don't even know. Ten, eleven years?"

"They live in Barcelona and you all live back in Brazil?"

"The official line is that they share time between Barcelona and Sao Paulo but..."

"Eleven years ago you were six." I said with no filter whatsoever.

I constantly get surprised about how other people's families work. I knew most people found it wild when they realised how young my mother was and how my godfathers and her raised me while they were also growing themselves. Even my dynamic with my stepfather is something wild to people who watch us, Avery says all the time we have chemistry us three, it just works, a perfect little family.

And I guess, I did love the way I was raised and I had no problem to say that my mother was definitely my best friend, which wasn't the case for most of the people I knew.

In a school like mine, they always wondered how I was so close to my parents when they were way more strict than the other parents.

"Marcela raised me." Augusto told me, "She's the one who probably would talk my ear off for going around New York drinking at stranger's houses."

I turned to him and found a clear, present free smile. "My Mam had me when she was sixteen."

Was it odd for me to offer such information out of the blue? Yes of course, but something in the way Augusto looked at me told me he connected the dots no problem.

"What's your theory?"

The words barely left my lips and the door suddenly opened and Avery, back in her normal clothes, came out, "Let's go, bitch, I'm hungry."

"Uber is waiting," Miles said tapping on his phone.

I nodded to my friends and turned back to Augusto, he shook his head.

"I'll tell you next time."

I agreed, and only when I was in the back seat of the car with Avery I stopped to think that there would never be next time.

CHAPTER ELEVEN

"I'm fine, Mam."

"Did you drink?"

"Just a little."

A huff, "You stayed glued to Avery and Miles?"

"Yes," I lied.

"Did you watch your glass all the time?"

"Mam. I'm fine. Repeat after me: London is fine!"

"Fuck's sake, London you were always a bit nerdy I was praying you'd never be invited to a party, ok?"

"Thanks Mam, that's just lovely of you."

"Don't blame a girl for dreaming. Tell me, was that Nathan guy there?"

I groaned, it was just after ten in the morning, Miles and Avery were still asleep together in Avery's bed, while I sneaked out to the bathroom to call Mam from Avery's phone. Mam wasn't impressed that I lost my phone, but I guaranteed her that it was all ok.

Something in me wasn't ready to explain the whole Nathan drama, I hadn't dealt with it yet and felt like telling Mam would put a weight on it that I wasn't ready for, so I simply said, "It was grand, we chatted a bit."

"Alright then," She didn't sound alright though, "When are you coming home?"

"Hmm, I was wondering if I could stay with Avery?"

"London…"

"Mam, we're just going to chill, ok? Miles is here too, watch a movie or whatever."

Mam cleared the back of her throat and I almost could hear the gears in her head turning. I wasn't lying to her. I was protecting her from the truth.

Last night everything that could go wrong went. The Nathan fiasco, losing my phone, getting separated from Miles and Avery… and still it worked out in the end right? So there you go, one more little bitty party wouldn't be a problem, right?

"Ok," she sighed, "But you need a new phone, girl. Can you get your ass down to a store and get one? Text me your new number after."

"Maybe someone at the party found it!" I protested, it felt excessive to buy a brand new phone a few hours after losing the old one.

"Sure, then you'll have two. I don't know if you realise but the only reason you have a phone is for me to know where you are all the time."

"You can call Avery or Miles."

"Get yourself a phone, London P."

I huffed and puffed, but eventually agreed and said my goodbyes. I wasn't against getting a new phone, it was just the hassle to go out of my way to purchase one that annoyed me.

When I was back in the room, both my friends were awake, talking about the events of the parties while eating last night's pizza in bed.

"How was Tina's party?" Avery asked when I sat with them and got a slice of the cold pizza.

"Obnoxious," I chewed on the vegan pizza that they never minded to order.

"Carol H said it was Wizard of Oz themed?"

"Yes, Tina fancied herself as being Judy Garland."

"Oh she definitely could take that role even further," Avery mocked in the perfect stupid accent Tina used last night.

"Who was your friend?" Miles wanted to know, "From the party last night."

"Augusto helped me to escape Nathan's serenade."

And I told them everything since we parted ways, my whole interaction with Nathan - that not in any way, shape or form gave him the right to sing a song about it, and everything with Augusto.

"I want to know his theory," Avery mused, "Do you think it's a sexy theory?"

I laughed, "I don't know, I think he was just goofing around…"

"Yes, a tall beautiful man comes to your rescue for a whole night and of course you think he's messing."

"I just..." I shook my head, "You know what Avery Nair? I won't be seeing him again so it really doesn't matter. Tell me what's the next party?"

To this, Avery stood up with a lot of energy for someone who was drinking and dancing just a few hours ago, "It's Bonnie's Pool party this afternoon."

"She's excited because Millie will be there," Miles informed me.

"Ahh I see."

Millie was older than us, she graduated last year and Avery had the biggest crush on her. When we were all in the school together it felt silly that someone like Millie would even look at Avery, but things changed and Avery have gotten much more confident. I knew she was salivating for a chance to be socially in the same place as Millie.

"And I have the opportunity not only to be drinking with her, but to be in a glorious bikini around her," Avery literally skipped her way to her closet and came back with the tiniest little pink bikini with a golden pattern.

"You know brown girls look dead drop gorgeous in pink," She said, doing a little dance that had me and Miles laughing.

"So Avery will finally hook up with Millie Rose," Miles said, "And it's the end of an era, because she will get over Millie in two seconds..."

Avery fake gasped and threw her bikini bottoms at Miles, but we all knew it was true. Avery was in love at least six times a year. It was entertaining if nothing more.

"I have nothing to wear, you know?" I told

Avery from the bed, getting a second slice of pizza, "And I need coffee."

Avery went to her closet and then threw at me a black string bikini still with the tags, "I knew you were going to play that card, bitch."

"We can smell London's nonsense a mile away," Miles informed me.

I made a face at him and looked at the bikini, it was far too small and I looked up to Avery, "You know I'm far too Irish to be wearing this shit, right?" Avery completely ignored me and turned the music on making Miles laugh.

Soon I got my wish and went to the kitchen to find coffee and had a super nice chat with Avery's mom, who was the nicest woman in town. Later we all had showers and Avery insisted on makeup even though it was a pool party.

"Bring a change of clothes because we have Tyler, Jack and Giovanni's parties later."

I stopped and looked at her, watching her apply blush on her cheek, "Tell me it is just one party."

"Nope, three."

"So we have four parties today? We can't possibly go to four parties in a day."

"You can sleep when you're dead, London," my infuriating best friend said.

"I might be dead by the end of this weekend."

"There's thirteen parties scheduled," Miles told me from the other side of the room.

"We can't possibly go to thirteen parties!"

"Well, there's only ten now, right?" Avery is still more concerned with her makeup than my little hissy fit.

"Tell you what, Jake's party is rumoured to be shit and you guys know I hate the basketball team…" Miles was saying and me and Avery agreed, "So we cut that one and make it twelve. 'Cause you know, it's Christmas."

I rolled my eyes, "Twelve is still a lot."

"It's only nine now…" Avery sang and Miles snickered.

"Why don't you put on a bikini and I'll worry about our social obligations?"

"I have to go out to get a new phone. Mam's orders."

"Ok, you do that then and meet us at the party in let's say two hours?" Avery made eye contact through the mirror and only stopped when I nodded.

I threw my bikini on, and a grey checked dress, black turtleneck and a chunk belt on top, which felt very odd over the bikini's strings. Tights and boots and I was ready.

CHAPTER TWELVE

London: This is my new number.

Mam: Good. Are you staying with Miles and Avery?

London: Yes, Mam.

Mam: Stop making me feel like I'm being annoying..

London: You're not annoying me.

Mam: That doesn't sound sincere…

London: Go annoy Emmet, Mam.

I snickered at the offended emoji Mam sent next while I ubered my way to Bonnie's house. I decided it was best just to get in an uber so I didn't need to look for the most ridiculous house on the road.

It was another yet big house but in the light of day looked even more out of my league. I saw a couple of people from school having a cigarette right in front of the door when I arrived and I noticed there were many more familiar faces than at the other parties, maybe because Bonnie was smart enough to pick a time where no other parties were happening.

I went through the house to find people scattered around the rooms, some in street clothes, some with damp skin and swimming costumes.

I looked around and started to get annoyed. If I was there before Avery and Miles I was going to flip.

Going through the kitchen, where a group were chatting away, I felt the exact moment when my stomach dropped and my eyes widened.

"How the hell do you know this many people in New York City?"

Augusto turned with that same easy smile playing on his lips, like he wasn't surprised at all by me by the kitchen door with a hand on my hips, "Now you want to hear my theory?"

I giggled like a total idiot but no one I knew was there to see. And when I say no one, I mean no one. Augusto had a completely different group around him and I was truly struggling to understand how someone from another country managed to know so many different people (and be invited to this many parties while he was at it).

"Does your theory have anything to do with the fact you are following me?"

He shook his head slowly and put the cup he had down, and without saying anything to the people around him, which I thought was a little rude, he came over to me and in a blink I was following him out of the kitchen.

"A couple of people I know told me about a few things going on today."

"So it's a complete coincidence?"

"Kind of."

I stopped in my tracks and arched an eyebrow, Augusto chuckled, "I hoped you would be here."

I looked from one side to the other, to the weird mix of dressed and undressed people. I didn't know where the indoor pool was, but I simply followed where most people seemed to be coming from.

"So tell me."

We passed an especially wet couple and I started to think we were going in the right direction, but I stopped straight away when he said:

"I think we're going to be meeting again and again."

I frowned, "What do you mean?"

"I think it's our thing," he shrugged, "You know, it's one of those stories."

"This is only the second day."

"But the third party in a row."

I shook my head and continued to walk, "But we clearly have similar groups of friends."

"But you don't think it's a little weird? Not even a little bit?"

I thought he was mad for a second, but I couldn't miss the laughing quality in his voice, "You're joking."

"Not necessarily. I tell you what, we are going to meet tomorrow," And extending his hand to me, "I bet you we will."

I stopped once more, looking down to his hand

and then to his coy smile, "If I'm right?"

"You're never going to see me again."

"If you're right?"

"I get your phone number."

I scoffed, "I thought we would meet regardless."

"We will, but we can make life much easier, can't we?"

I didn't know him, I reminded myself. Simply as it was, we met last night I confirmed to myself, even though the banter made it feel like he knew me better. Which was such nonsense, there weren't enough eyerolls in the world.

He accompanied me after Nathan's fiasco and made sure I was safe and with my friends. Maybe it was one of those things that you can't go through together without getting a little attached.

I started walking, ignoring his attempt to shake on it. I heard Augusto's big laugh behind me, "What part of my theory you don't believe?"

"The whole part!" I said trying to sound indignant but I was a little amused, "I'm still worrying you're following me on purpose."

"Do you think I asked around if you were going to be at this party?"

"I…" I opened my mouth and he pressed one more time, "Who knew you would be here?"

Hmm. Well, only Avery and Miles and until the morning not even my mother knew I was going to come. So who could he have asked? God knew the amount of shenanigans with my school peers, he would need to go to ten parties before finding the right one.

"And you think it is a complete coincidence we keep meeting?"

"I know it's a coincidence, but now I think we will keep meeting like this…"

"Until when?" I asked looking up to him.

"Until you meet me on purpose."

I laughed and shook my head, when I wasn't being implicant just for the fun of it I did appreciate the silliness of the whole thing. We finally reached a closed door beside the home gym, if you could guess where an indoor pool is, wouldn't you bet beside the gym?

I opened the door, and not thinking twice, closed it immediately.

I felt the tips of my toes to the very last strand of my hair turning a very particular shade of red, I bit the side of my mouth and in the quickest turn of my life I started to walk back.

Augusto had a two second delay to understand what was happening, but after a moment he jogged after me.

"What's going on?"

"That wasn't the place."

"What was there?"

I shook my head and felt my cheeks turning redder and redder. He tried to stop me but I kept walking, I would walk to my own house if I had to.

"What the hell you saw to make you…"

And suddenly he stopped, and for some reason that felt worse to me, so I stopped too. "Let's go," I said over gritted teeth.

"I want to go back and have a look at what the hell made you turn that shade of red," He turned as he was going back and I threw my body in front of him.

"You don't want to see that."

"I don't know... I'm really curious..." he said in a light voice, not really making any effort to pass through me, "Maybe if you tell me..."

I rolled my eyes, "There were people..." Red again, Jesus Christ, "People from my school and they..."

Obviously Augusto finally understood the nature of the scene I just saw, and I could see his understanding by the slow smile growing on his face.

"Tell me."

"Believe me I'm working hard in forgetting all about it. Going to school is painful enough."

He chuckled again but when his gaze passed over me I knew he was way too curious for his own good.

"I won't share names..." I informed him, because, while I was very traumatised I did not believe in spreading any type of rumours being them truthful or not, "But I can say... There were four of them."

Augusto whistled and shook his head, "Man, your school knows how to party."

CHAPTER THIRTEEN

"It's you again! London, it's him. Again!"

"I've noticed, Ave."

"It is a coincidence?" Avery asked Augusto.

"Yes," he answered promptly.

"We'll see," I said right after.

"You look tense."

Avery, on the other hand, never looked so relaxed, showing off her pink and golden bikini, spread on the smaller part of the pool with her silky hair piled on top of her head.

Turned out that the real pool was in the closest part of the house and so damn easy to get to, different from the sauna beside the gym where I was before.

Just thinking of it made me red and itchy. Listen, I'm not a prude, but you can all agree seeing your classmates in that position...

Ugh. I tried to let it go, swallowing past my silly

embarrassment.

"Are you changing?" She blinked at me.

I felt like I was about to faint under my turtleneck, tights and boots. The steamy pool created mist all over us and it felt hard to breathe, however the last thing I wanted was to sit down and relax there.

Avery frowned when I shook my head, and before I could come up with an excuse, Augusto was the one who talked, "Let's just get a drink first."

Avery looked at him like he saw him for the first time, "Would you ever sing 'More than Words' to her?"

"AVERY!"

"I don't know how to sing," he said simply, not really guaranteeing anything.

I shook my head and faced Avery, "I'll come back in a minute then, are you staying put?"

Her gaze slid to the right side in the middle of a bunch of girls where Millie was laughing, "Yes," And was the biggest yes of all times, I chuckled.

We left the pool area and I could breathe for the first time, the colder air calming my lungs. We walked in silence for a bit, both of us breathing deeply, I turned left into the kitchen and I went straight for a can of coke inside a bucket full of ice at one side of the next room.

"What's the matter?" I asked Augusto when I caught his stare.

"That's a good question, what's the matter?"

I shrugged.

"I only saw you having fun for a second last night, and well, most of it you were worried to find your friends and annoyed with that guy but now…"

I looked at him and shook my head and then jumped up and sat on the table.

"It's a lot of work, isn't it? Feels like a lot of work."

"What?"

I looked around, "This whole thing. You know what, I'm always back in Ireland for the holidays and it always felt like I was missing something…"

He nodded like I made total sense, "There's a little tiresome quality in everyone here. Like that girl? Tina?"

I shook my hands enthusiastically and he laughed, "That's exactly what I am talking about! She's nice enough, and gorgeous… Rich. Why can't her party just be a party? Why does it need to be freaking flying monkeys in front of her house? What the hell?"

He laughed and laughed more than I thought was normal but suddenly I was laughing too. We looked at each other, and one would say "flying monkey" and we were back at the beginning. It wasn't exactly funny, but it felt like the absurdity of the parties, the over the top behaviour of everyone was something we should laugh about.

"And now there's foursomes going on in the sauna…" I said once my voice was back, "Can people just have normal non-themed parties and have sex with the door locked?"

"I guess it's the party of the theatrics," he shrugged.

"Are the people from your school that ridiculous?"

He thought for a second, but eventually nodded, "In a less artistic way, I guess. But you know, everyone goes for a week in Mexico kind of situation."

"You know what, Mam had this ridiculous car back home and it was almost always on the brink of giving up. But every summer she would try to take at least a couple of days off and drive us somewhere. Even if we had to sleep in the car at the beach. They're my favourite memories."

Augusto nodded, "Maybe that's the thing. Some people don't have those kinds of memories so they tend to make events bigger and bigger to create unforgettable moments. You can't blame them for trying."

I took a sip from my can of coke, "I guess you're right."

"I'm always right."

I rolled my eyes, "Don't start."

"I'm not starting anything."

"I know you're thinking about fate and destiny…"

"That's far more elaborate than anything I've said…"

I opened my mouth to retort something snarky but suddenly the foursome, still damp from the sauna, arrived at the kitchen. I turned bright red and closed my mouth at once.

Augusto looked between me and the newcomers, once and twice and when he almost figured it out, I jumped off the table and dragged him by the sleeves outside.

CHAPTER FOURSOME

I texted Miles saying I left and not even two seconds later I got a text from Avery absolutely disgusted. I paid no attention, it was clear that my bad mood wasn't just themed party related, but coming from a lack of proper food and sleep.

"Where are you going?" he asked and I told him my address without thinking much about it.

"Ok, that's not far from my hotel, I can go with you."

"I don't need a babysitter, you know. It's bright in the middle of the day, and I know my way home."

"I know you know," He shrugged, "How many blocks from here?"

I thought for a second, I wouldn't walk normally, getting an uber was definitely the way to go, but at the same time, it was a nice enough day and fresh air would do me good.

"It's not far. But it's a walk."

"Let's go!"

He had a little pep in his step that made me laugh, and he joined me.

"How about I use this walk to explain my theory?"

I couldn't stop myself, I rolled my eyes again.

"Aw, come on. Only as long as we are walking."

I didn't say a word, but I nodded.

He clapped his gloved hands and rubbed them together, "So yes, I do believe that we are meant to meet again and again. And I have a few reasons to believe that, would you care to hear it?"

I chuckled and waved my hand in front of us as the one who gives permission, "You might as well."

"I wasn't supposed to go to that party. Yes, I knew a few people, but I made a mistake and went to the wrong place. But once I was there and I texted my brother and he wasn't there I decided to have a drink and listen to the band anyway... But some jackass started to play some cheesy song."

I laughed and he continued:

"I mean, I could argue that we were meant to meet just based on the fact that I had no one there and you kept bumping with me all the time."

"I'm sorry."

"That's all right," He said in a very nice way, like it was really all right.

"So not just that, but then right when I think I'm never going to see you again? There you are, waiting in line for the bathroom," And like I didn't understand his point, he had to make it obvious,

"Fate."

"I told you, you clearly have connections with people that know people from my school. It's not that unbelievable that…"

"What about just now? This party just now? I wasn't with Dante!"

I frowned and turned to him, "That's true. Who the hell you knew then?"

He waved me away, "Some of Carlos' buddies…"

He tried to dismiss it but I jumped into action:

"That's what I'm telling you! It's all the same group of friends. It's a little obvious that we will meet eventually."

"London, I can't believe you are a non believer."

My mouth broke in the most sincere laughter and I shook my head, "You met me literally five minutes ago."

"And yet we've been through so much…"

That made me giggle again, he noticed and bumped into me in a friendly way, "I think we are one of those people that will meet again and again. You know the type of person you manage to meet in the middle of the biggest city and…"

I looked at him with an eyebrow raised, he smiled and pointed at me, "Exactly. We managed to meet three times in the last forty eight hours in New York City! Think about that for just a second…"

"Ok, sure, but even if that's true… What's the end? We just will bump into each other forever and ever?"

Augusto brought his hand to his chin, like he

really needed to think about that one, "No, I guess it stops once you agree to see me on purpose."

"Or you go back to Brazil."

"Nah, I doubt that would be a problem."

I made a face more to myself, putting my hands deep into my coat while we crossed a busy street.

"Are you just a bullshitter or do you really believe in that type of stuff?"

"A little of both," he shrugged, "It's a half joke when I talk about fate… But I do believe some people are able to attract another. Over and over again."

I bit my lip thinking about that, about Mam and Emmet and all they went through to be together. I lived in the Montgomery-Scott house, I couldn't just dismiss a little thing called destiny, could I?

"Don't you think it's a little fun to believe in nonsense sometimes?" He asked waking me up from my day dream.

I thought about that one, "Maybe… But it feels like cheating if we know it's bullshit."

"But everything is half truth half a lie. Like you put a goal for yourself and you want it to be true, but you also know that might not happen because of many reasons…"

"So we can believe it's maybe fate, but it might be not in case there's no such a thing as fate."

"Exactly."

I stepped in front of him, a big toy store beside us, Christmas decorations everywhere. People coming and going with big bags full of wrapped gifts. It was like we stopped right in the middle of a Christmas movie.

"So let's try again. Tonight. Test it out."

It seemed like he was put off by it, but when I extended my hand between us, Augusto took and shook it.

"I'll go to a party tonight," I said, "And maybe I'll see you there."

He winked, "You'll see me there."

I twisted my lips, our hands still holding one another, I looked it down to them and then up to him, "No messages, no clues from anyone."

"Decide on a party and go, tell no one. Not even Avery."

I should point out that I felt like this was the most unsafe and weirdest bet I've ever been involved in, but at the same time I couldn't back out. I wasn't sure if it was because I wanted to prove him wrong, or if I wanted him to be right. Probably because in a very real way I just wanted to see him again and it was a strange thing to confess to myself about someone I met not even two days ago.

"See you tonight," He said certainly and I nodded and finally let his hand go.

I stepped back, and then again. I wasn't exactly home and he didn't ask to follow me until I reached my destination, we just nodded to each other, and I turned around and looked at the ground until I got home.

CHAPTER FIFTEEN

"And all went well… The end."

Mam huffed and started to follow me around, driving me insane. That woman could smell my lies, she knew the party had not gone so well if I wasn't dying to go about the details, but I was hoping she wasn't suspecting I was lying about the whole thing.

Especially when I wanted to go to another party this evening.

I passed the sitting room and the kitchen, the hall and went for my room with Will on my heels and Mam right after. I sat on my bed first, then Will and then Mam. We both scratched the dog at the same time.

"Liar, liar, pants on fire," she sang.

Mam was relentless, that's something everyone knew. She would bug the life out of me until I just stopped and gave her the full version.

"I met Nathan there," I told her and I swear she even sat straighter, "And we were having a great night, and chatting and then he said he was going to get us drinks…"

"I will be interrupting the story to say that you *never* let anyone touch your drink besides yourself…"

"I know, I know, listen… He never went to get the drinks."

Mam's hand found her mouth, "Oh, god, he just left you there?"

"Worse."

"You saw him kissing another girl?"

I chuckled, "Worse."

"What the fuck, London, is he married with three kids?"

I laughed at that one, "He went up the stage and dedicated a song to me."

"A song?"

"Yes, a goddamn song."

"What song?"

"More than Words."

Mam winced, I laughed a little because if nothing, it was a funny story after all.

"Could be worse," she said but I saw the little curving of her lips.

"How could it possibly be worse than this?"

"Wonderwall?"

I threw a pillow on her, scaring the life out of Will, and Mam caught it mid-air.

"Ok, it's weird…"

"Mam, is more than weird."

"It's really more than words…" She laughed openly and I threw my other pillow, which this time hit her square on the face.

"We never kissed, we never had a proper date!" I wined, "He sang to me in front of my whole school!"

"The whole school?"

"Not the whole school… but you know…"

"Let me see it…" She asked all of the sudden and I frowned at her, so she said it again, "Can I see him singing?"

"What do you mean…"

I saw the moment when she realised I had no idea what she was talking about, a flash of understanding and suddenly she was up.

"Ok then, you better have a shower and rest a little uh?"

"What do you mean by letting you see it?"

"I was going to make soup for dinner!" She clapped her hands like anyone gave a damn about soup.

"Mam…"

A sigh and she shook her head, "It was a big party with a bunch of teenagers. I just assumed someone had a video of it, ok?"

I knew my face paled instantly, I never thought about a video. Why hadn't I thought about it??

I opened my bag looking for my new phone while Mom was talking non-stop, "I was just assuming shit, Lon, I'm probably wrong!"

I scoffed at her, we both knew she never was so right in her entire life. I got my phone and of course I had no apps yet. No damn Instagram, which was the first thing I downloaded.

"I know people filmed it but now what?" I asked her while I waited.

"You need to say it was a lovely gesture but you guys aren't together. Just be polite about it."

"Everyone is going to think we are together, it doesn't matter what I say. I'm never going to date again!"

"I heard celibacy does wonders for the skin, maybe we should get one of those rings for you…"

One mean look from me and she shut her mouth at once.

I finally was able to type in my login and for a second nothing came up, and I let out a breath. It didn't last long though, because suddenly it showed how many times I was tagged in a video.

One, two, three… ten versions of the same video from different angles. Some caught what he said in the beginning, some were just a short part of the song. A few of them had floating hearts and called Nathan a dream, another few had my name and Nathan's after #relationshipgoals. But then there were the people, the ones who believed that was the cruellest thing that ever happened to a student, and boy, they were vocal about it.

I was tagged on the third meme when Mom took the phone out of my hand, "It doesn't matter."

I opened my mouth, but Mam was already shaking her head, "It doesn't matter."

I frowned but it got soft, and I breathed in and out, Mama's hands on mine, "People say all kinds of shit," She smiled.

If anyone knew how to handle people saying things behind her back was Mam. I nodded and got calmer, she was right, sure, it was more than annoying, but in the big scheme of things? It didn't really matter.

"You've talked to him since?"

I shook my head.

"Ok, maybe you should have a talk and explain you're not in the same place as he is?"

The understatement of the year, but I nodded anyway.

"So he was a little crazier than we thought…" She giggled and I followed suit, "Big deal. I've seen crazier!"

I bet she did and for no good reason whatsoever, but maybe if Mam would feel sorry for me that would be the time, I asked:

"There's another thing going on today. Can I go?"

"What's a thing?"

I shrugged, "A party kind of thing."

"Hmm…"

"Don't I get a voucher because yesterday was rubbish?"

Mam laughed, "Jesus, you're full of shit. Alright, Emmet is bringing you and collecting you, though."

I opened my mouth, but she was shaking her head and wagging her finger at me.

"You won't be partying around New York City like I have no common sense, London P."

"Ok," I said exasperated.

But let's be honest, a ride wasn't the worst deal.

CHAPTER SIXTEEN

Even if he was discreet, I could feel Emmet's eye on me while he drove me to the next party.

I moved around in the seat, my skin feeling prickly, I wanted to scratch my cheek and all over the hairline. I cracked my fingers, one after the other.

Another look. He knew something was bothering me.

But how could I explain? How could I tell him I asked my best friend for the addresses of all parties happening today and I gave him one of those addresses and even Avery didn't know each party I was going to attend?

I didn't know.

How could I tell my stepfather he was driving to someone's house, with maybe no friends just because a guy I met the other day thinks we are destined to meet.

I counted blue cars, one, two three. I still wanted to scratch all over my face, but I was aware the itch wasn't physical, it came from the oddness of being this carefree person. A girl that may or may not believe in destiny.

But I didn't of course, I wasn't that dumb.

Still I was in the car, still I followed the rules of our game and I was sure the only reason was because I actually liked to play. That never happened before, I never found the strong willingness to be part of anything.

"Just tell me one thing, ok?"

I turned my head to Emmet and frowned. I almost forgot he was splitting his time between driving and watching me.

"And what is that?"

"I know you won't tell me what's going on,"

I opened my mouth, but my stepfather chuckled and raised his hand, "I know you well, kid."

I nodded, he did know me well, apparently as well as anyone. At times even more than Mam, simply because Mam had a lot of expectations and hopes for me, while Emmet just observed. He took everything at face value, he never questioned what was happening in front of him, and at the moment when I presented all the signs I was uncomfortable, he took that close to his chest.

"Just let me know how much I need to worry. Scale one to ten?"

"Zero."

"London…"

"I'm not playing. I'm being… dumb. There's nothing to worry about."

To my surprise, he nodded, "Alright then. You can text me later and let me know if I need to start worrying."

I giggled because that was a very Emmet thing to say, always calm and never judgmental. I wish he stopped worrying though, what I was doing felt silly but I wasn't in any type of danger.

Especially if I actually met Augusto.

I breathed deep when Emmet stopped the car and pointed to a posh building a few numbers down the road, "That's it."

I nodded, feeling ever so silly, he reminded, "Just call me anytime when you want to come home, ok?"

"I'm surprised Mam didn't give me a curfew."

"Well, I think she's testing you. You know, see if you're responsible when left to your own devices."

I scoffed, "And I was here giving her credit…"

Emmet looked at me, serious, but I could still spot humour in his eyes, "Don't drink alcohol, don't leave your cup down. Stay around people you know and call me anytime and all times."

"Thanks Emily," I called him by his nickname and left the car.

"I love you, kid," he said when I closed the door and made a face, he laughed, it was fine.

I made my way to the party I didn't know I was going to, texting Avery quickly I showed her the address asking, "*Who's party is this?*"

"Mackenzie and Lee," she texted back, "That's where you are?"

I simply said "Yes" and put the phone back in my bag. I was glad to have picked a party of someone somewhat nice, I had a few classes with Lee and he was an okay person, his twin Mackenzie seemed to be nice as well.

Dressed in a uniform, the doorman did not ask where I was going, or even bother to ask for my name. I was sure he knew about the party and asking for every teenager's name probably got tedious at some point.

What he told me was, "Penthouse," without taking his eye off the paper he was reading. I gave a tiny "thank you", but I wasn't sure if he heard me.

In the lift, the feeling of stupidity came in a crushing wave. Why would I ever do something like this? I barely liked parties, but Avery and Miles made it better. However, I was alone, by my own design. And just after I found out that Nathan's song was all over the internet. It seemed rather silly to be out there, with no one by my side, no armour to face the other humans.

My foot tapped on the lift's floor and echoed around me. Stupid, stupid, stupid.

I made that silly bet with Augusto but it almost escaped me that if he wasn't around I would need to be with a lot of people. I wasn't sure I wanted to know what he thought of me.

The lift opened right in the middle of the sitting room, like a goddamn dream.

Christ on a bike, I knew a lot of wealthy people, but that was just damn silly.

The sitting room spread with a big chandelier right in the middle, the view of Manhattan was breathtaking. Blue lights, low pop music and something a little more human about this party, like even though it was clearly from someone with money, it didn't have a theme. Finally just a party was enough.

I was dressed in black skinny jeans with a bunch of holes, which I started to pick at while waiting like a moron just by the lift. I was glad this time around I decided to wear a chunky jumper, it was like protection for me somehow.

One foot after the other, it would be a lie if I didn't say I tried my best not to look around. Because then I could be surprised, then he can find me instead of the other way around.

I got to the free bar and ordered a vodka lime, my foot tapping again, my head down and I never felt so stupid.

Why was I even there? I should just go.

Wait.

I should give it a lap, check if Augusto was anywhere, make peace with the non destiny of our lives and call Emmet. If there was someone in the whole world who wouldn't make a fuss for me to call ten minutes after arriving, that was Emmet.

The vodka lime was in front of me and I took the first sip praying for liquid courage, which was silly, I reminded myself. I didn't need any type of courage, I could just leave.

I nodded to myself deciding on giving a lap before announcing the complete fiasco of a night, but my front bumped to a chest, my vodka lime soaked us both.

I gasped and curse, and he said:

"Can we talk?"

CHAPTER SEVENTEEN

Nathan led me to the balcony and I was dead set on pretending people weren't following us with their gossip hungry eyes.

He looked as nice as always, tall, high cheekbones... wholesome. This time around his features looked tough though, painfully uncomfortable.

I swallowed dryly. Nathan looked at me and to the window beside us with all the people watching us and he winced. I didn't dare to look.

"I tried to call you..." Nathan started and I shook my head, the apology coming out before anything else, "I lost my phone!" And I took my new phone out of my bag, "I got a new one today."

Nathan hummed and I wondered if he thought I would buy a whole new phone just to avoid his messages. What a crazy thing to do.

"A phone conversation would be better than this…" He murmured signalling again to the double glass windows just beside us.

I shuffled on my feet, my hands were damp and gross. I didn't do awkward, I wasn't cool like Miles or quick on my feet like Avery. I was sarcastic, which with time I learned many people would take the wrong way if they didn't know me enough, and god I was sure Nathan did not know me at all.

I opened my mouth but no sound came out, so I closed it again. I saw Nathan raising his hand and scratching his cheek and I wished a meteor would arrive to end this cringy conversation.

"I guess you're clearly alright and the reason you left was because you didn't like the song…"

My eyes widened and I looked at him, open mouthed. God, I never thought about that part did I? I never for one second had the decency to think that simply leaving with no phone on top of it all could make Nathan think something was wrong with me.

I felt my whole body tingle with regret, and shame washed all over me. I was plenty of things, but never selfish.

"I'm sorry, Nathan," I said, frowning to myself, "I was just overwhelmed and didn't think about…"

"Me."

Shit. He was right, I guessed, it was so stupid for some many reasons. Leaving him and my friends behind, going with a stranger, having no phone and no way to talk to anyone.

I sighed, what was done was done, and while I did feel extremely ashamed I couldn't do anything about it.

"I'm sorry for leaving you. I could have stayed and explained myself," so proud of my maturity.

"And what would be the explanation?"

Oh.

I never…

Damn.

"London?"

I nodded, yes, of course, he wanted to know the truth, because to him singing a song to someone in the middle of a first date is the normal thing to do. Something that was supposed to make me swoon I guessed.

"It was a little…" I really tried to look for a better word for it, but in the end I only shrugged and ended up saying, "much."

Nathan stepped back like a slapped him, "I was being romantic…"

"I know… I know that you thought…"

"Not just me. Many people watched and…"

Oh man, I suddenly remembered how many people were there that night, many of them probably watching our conversation at that exact minute. I remembered the videos on Instagram and the comments and while I did believe it was very irresponsible of me to just leave with Augusto I couldn't just swallow the bullshit that he thought singing like that on our first date was proper behaviour.

"We…" shaking my head, "We never even kissed before, Nathan…. And you just…"

"I thought it was going well…"

"It was going well!"

"Not that well if…"

I shook my head again, "It was going well. I was very much into you, but you left to sing the tackiest song ever…"

Oh, fuck.

So Nathan was one of those people who felt very offended when their musical taste was questioned, I could see by his outraged expression.

"It's just not my taste?" And it came out as doubtful as I felt. I wanted to soften the blow but Nathan wasn't having it, not after I called the song tacky.

"It's an excellent song and many people said…"

"Nathan…" I breathed out, "Maybe that's the problem. You never asked me, you never knew what I thought about being serenaded in the middle of our first date. Or even my musical taste. You didn't know…"

"Yes! Because it was our first date and…"

"It wasn't even our first date! We met at a party and we were having a great time and…" I was trying to find the best words to express how I was feeling and tiptoe around his feelings, "If you had stayed you would know better about me."

I had nothing else to say because that was the bottom line. We saw each other at school and, besides a few short sentences, Lisa's party was the first time Nathan and I had a full conversation, and he was right, it was going well but it felt wild to me that his instincts were to go up on a stage and call my name.

"Maybe that's for the best," I shrugged hopefully, "we figured out something about each other early on…"

His dry laugh chilled my bones and I wondered where the self proclaimed romantic had gone?

Nathan moved towards the glass door and I followed his motion. I couldn't not see the people looking at us through the glass, even those dancing had their eyes on me.

My ears grew red, I had to leave that party, I needed to be out of that mess as quickly as possible.

"I'm sorry anyway," I said when he opened the door.

"Whatever."

And that was that. I wasn't feeling sad exactly. Nathan was a crush, sure, but I wasn't in love with him, he never gave me the chance to meet him properly. I was a little ashamed for never even considering how it felt for him to be left behind that night, but if I was being honest, what I felt the most was the exhaustion of the night.

It was a complete fiasco, Augusto wasn't anywhere to be found and suddenly I started to blame myself for everything.

Again, this was just the consequences of my own choices. I was a logical person and I let him convince me fate was such a thing and I went to a party completely alone for no good reason.

Shaking myself out of my stupor I left the cold balcony, and parted the crowd going straight to the lift.

I heard people calling my name but my curt smile and short nod must have shown them I wasn't good company anymore, and when the lift door closed with me inside and the music was muffled, I breathed easily.

Texting Emmet quickly and asking for a ride,

my stepfather once more came through by simply saying "Alright" and not asking anything else. He should teach Mam a thing or two.

My normal instincts were to take my phone and look down to it to pretend I was doing something, but instead I watched the night.

The doorman asked if I liked to order a cab, but I shook my head and said I was waiting for a ride, he was nice enough to be outside with me, it was the type of gentle care that brought a smile to my face and made me feel safer, I thanked him in a low voice.

And while the city lights danced and a soft white snow started to come down on us, I heard the rushed footsteps crossing the street.

I shook my head when he said, "Still counts!"

"I'm waiting for my lift."

Augusto came close to me, his cheeky smile almost melted the snow around us, "I made just one mistake."

"Were you in the wrong party?"

"It doesn't matter, I got here."

"Late," I said but with a smile playing on my lips.

"I came through, though. We are here, right now."

I tried to stop my smile, I wanted to pretend he wasn't as charming as he thought he was, but I couldn't stop myself.

It was a long short night and playing around with him was everything I wanted.

I watched Emmet's car park at the same place he left me not long ago and I turned to Augusto again.

"My ride's here."

"Stay…"

I wanted to, but I was also tired and a lot of feelings surfaced since my talk with Nathan. In the end I wasn't the best person to be around.

"I'm sorry…" It was my official line for the night, but Augusto shook his head and never lost his smile.

"We'll try again tomorrow."

"What?" I laughed, "This did not end well!"

"Of course it did. I found you, I can find you tomorrow too."

I nodded while I walked to Emmet's direction, Augusto shot my way the brightest smile I've seen and what a surprise when I got into the car, I had a very similar one stamped on my face.

CHAPTER EIGHTEEN

"So tell me again. You only met him a few nights ago?"

I faced frontwards to avoid Avery's eager smile, "At Lisa's party. You know this, I told you already."

"I know, I know… it just feels odd coming from you."

I turned to her with an expression I knew was showing alarm, "There's nothing bad about it," my best friend said, shaking her head and laughing, "I like the energy of the whole thing. Very When Harry Met Sally."

I said nothing, waiting patiently in line for our coffees, Avery elbowed me, "I think it's cute."

I groaned, she laughed and grabbed my hand, "So you think he will find you?"

"I think he's silly enough to try."

I smiled. How did I get there? A few nights ago

Nathan was the only boat on the horizon and now that was done and dusted, and Augusto just introduced himself to my life and brought so much... fun to it. How fun was it to be this silly?

To think that we would find each other in the middle of New York City, the absurdity that for some reason this guy from Brazil who I met five minutes ago could have his destiny intertwined with mine?

It was delusion, silly and just plain fun.

"I think he's right, you know?"

"About what?" I turned to her.

She shrugged, "It's very odd if you think about it, you know? You guys keep bumping into each other..."

"It wasn't that many times...."

"They were enough times," a voice came from just behind us, and when I turned he was there, of course he was.

I said, "That doesn't count!" at the same time he said, "It does count!"

"We said tonight," I argued like a fool.

Augusto smiled easily like he always did and turned to Avery, "Hey Avery."

"Hi handsome," she replied, being so very relaxed in her own skin.

We ordered at our turn and Augusto added a coffee for himself while chatting with Avery and once our order was ready he looked at me, "Come with me."

"With you?"

Avery walked ahead of us towards the exit and I was happy, since Augusto was giving me the eyes and I was starting to melt a little. I didn't need anyone to see it, especially Avery.

"Yes," he insisted, "Spend the day with me."

We left the shop to the cold street with my steamy coffee in hand and I looked up to him with an inevitable smile.

Shit, aren't we in trouble?

"Come on, I've found you."

He did, didn't he? He freaking did it.

Augusto took my hand on his and tugged, I laughed and my feet were following him before my mind made a decision.

"Ok, kids, you guys have fun," Avery was saying going the opposite way from us.

She never asked anything, never made me say out loud that of course I was going with him. Not Avery, she was just on board it didn't matter what I decided, she was the type of friend who knows best.

Avery wiggled her fingers at us and crossed the street with a knowing smile.

"Where are we going?"

"I made no plans. I didn't know I was going to see you."

Augusto held my hand tightly, guiding us through the last minute shoppers, "We can play a game."

"What kind of game?"

He looked at me and then in front, "Ok, right or left?"

"What?"

"You need to answer the first thing that comes to mind for this to work! Right or left, London?"

I giggled, "Left!"

And we turned left, so he told me, "I choose

right"

So we turned on the next right. We played the game for a couple of more turns, until he asked me to choose a number between one and five, so I squeaked "Four!" like an overly excited toddler.

Augusto twirled me around to face our destiny, pun intended. We were just in front of a beautiful vintage looking independent bookshop and the most gorgeous tabby cat was sitting at the window watching us.

I smiled and looked up to Augusto who tugged me to the shop's direction, "Let's go…"

I opened the bookstore's door and the cute bells made me so very happy. The place was breathtaking, the kind of jewel in the middle of the city, a place I would never find on my own, not when we are so used to going to the same places all the time.

The gorgeous rolls and rolls of dark wood shelves packed with books was a dream come true. The cat from the window hadn't moved but a black one passed in front of us…

I turned to my right and saw a cute blonde one and to my left a Siamese passing with so much pomp that only they can have. My mouth fell agape and I tightened my grip on Augusto's arm.

"It's one of those cat book shops!"

I was very aware how high my voice was coming out but I couldn't stop myself. It was like a dream come true, like something you say would be great to visit but never really make the time.

The woman behind the counter with a messy silver bun on top of her head and more necklaces than I could count, offered a kind smile but pointed at our cups:

"No drinks inside the shop, kids."

We nodded and I promptly threw my and his cup at the bin in front of us trying my best not to disturb the owner or the beautiful cats.

I walked through the first shelf which held the fantasy books, my favourite genre. My fingers touched each spine, one by one, some which I read, some that I didn't. A soft Persian cat jumped from somewhere to the top of the shelf I was looking at and watched me with its golden eyes.

I smiled and tentatively went to pet him and was satisfied when I was allowed.

"Will is going to be pissed at me…"

"Who's Will?"

I scrunch my nose, "My dog."

"Wil…" Augusto nodded like he approved my name choice so I helped him, "William Shakespeare."

"Oh…" He understood and chuckled, "That's a good name. You like books, then."

"Yes. We read a lot at home so…"

I felt a little shy, it was all banter between us but at that point when he was asking about me suddenly felt like… a real date.

"So…?"

I shook my head, the Persian cat got bored of us and skipped away, so I kept walking looking at the book titles, and I took one and showed to him, "This beauty has a love triangle between a girl, a boy and an AI who takes over the boy's body. That's good writing."

Augusto laughed, "Nothing better than a good love triangle. Especially when robots are involved…"

I waggled my finger at him, and put the book back in place, "Not a robot, he's an AI."

"Sorry."

I looked up to him and we both smiled right at the same time. I felt the butterflies right in my belly and I felt my cheeks and ears getting red.

How did that happen? How was it so easy and challenging at the same time? Every time we were together the conversation was flowing and it felt just perfect, but when I remembered the small... just the tiny fact that I had a crush on him...

That's when things got a little out of control.

"What do you think about when you get all flustered?"

Eyes widened and I almost choked on nothing but air.

"Come on..." He said in such a silky voice I...

I turned from him, passing along the shelves once more, "I don't know... I feel a tad awkward..."

"Why?"

"I don't know," I frowned, "I thought everyone got a little awkward from time to time?"

"Yes, sure, but when we met you seemed much more relaxed..."

"I had no awkward left in my body at that point!"

Augusto chuckled, I felt his thumb right in the inner side of my wrist and it made me a little light headed. From the base of my wrist, his thumb went up my arm and stopped right before my elbow, when he stopped, I was able to let a breath out.

"Nathan came to talk to me last night," I blurted out for no reason whatsoever like the nut job I was.

"Who?"

"The song guy."

Nodding, "The more than words guy…"

"Yes."

I said nothing else, the little black cat I'd seen before hopped close to my feet and I went down to pet it.

"So how was it?"

I stood up when the cat left and I wished he was still there to give me an excuse, it was me who started this conversation wasn't it? So what was my deal?

"Well, he pointed out how shitty it was of me to just leave… I think maybe he was worried…"

"Hmm… I get that."

"He's a nice person, I think."

"You think?"

Augusto came to stand just beside me, "I don't know him enough to be sure. But I think he actually thinks that was a thoughtful gesture… And…"

Augusto shook his head, "On a first date? In front of the whole school? I don't think so, I'm sorry."

I shrugged, "Whatever, that's not my problem anymore. I mean, people at school still think I'm dating him…"

"What have I told you about letting people say what they want to say?"

I chuckled, "Yeah, you're right."

Augusto looked down to me with a knowing smirk and to my surprise took my hand, "Go on now, I'm getting you a book, just tell me which one."

CHAPTER NINETEEN

I adjusted my earrings and looked at the mirror in silent thought. I decided to wear my favourite dress, a slip blue dress with a white plan t-shirt underneath, I was sure it was to bring me good luck.

I was biting inside my mouth and Will rolled from one side to the other right on top of my bed making a sad doggy sound. He had something nasty to eat and now was feeling a little icky.

A knock on my door while I was curling my hair and Mam got her head through the gap, "Can I come in?"

"Sure…"

She took no time in making herself comfortable on my bed with Will. Without looking she sat right on top of the book I left there and then, with a face, took it out from underneath her bum and read the title.

"I don't remember reading this…"

"It's a new one," I told her through the mirror.

She hummed but didn't ask anything else, thank god.

"So, another party…"

"The last party."

"There's been a lot of parties…"

"Yes, Mam, and now they're over."

"Are you feeling better about the whole Nathan thing?"

We looked at each other in the mirror and I smiled at her, taking my brushes and applying a little of makeup, "I guess it doesn't matter what people think."

"Hmm, that's a surprisingly mature attitude."

I frowned at her, "You told me that!"

Mam shrugged, "I know, I just never expected you to listen."

What I didn't tell her was Augusto told me something very similar but in a way more convincing way with a lot of more slow lovely smiles. I bit my bottom lip and tried to decide if I needed lipstick or not.

"Who's the man, Daughter Dearest?"

My head shot up and I made the most revealing and stupid worried face, Mam chuckled.

"Come on, I know you. Just tell me what's happening."

I turned on my chair and I looked at my Mam's face, she was beaming, the stupid smile of someone who got something right.

My mother is full of shit, everyone knows it, but it is very hard to hide things from her. She's smart and quick and registers everything around her like a little sponge. Mam can tell my moods, and Emmet's too but not just that, she can tell if something is wrong by just a hello, she knows all our secrets.

I start telling her about Augusto, avoiding the part that I fled the first party with him, just about the meeting all the time in random places and his theory of fate. Mam listened to every single thing I had to say in a focused silence and when I finished she asked:

"When he's leaving?"

The little balloon that formed inside my chest while I talked about Augusto burst right away. Mam noticed and I saw the moment she regretted.

"I'm sorry Lon…"

I shook my head and turned again back to the mirror looking for a lipstick I didn't really want.

"I was just wondering because you said he's here on holidays…"

"I know, Mam. It's fine. I don't know when he's going home."

I knew Mam hadn't said it to upset me, she wasn't the type of person to rain on anyone's parade. My brain knew it, but my heart still felt offended that she had the courage to bring it up because at the end of the day, how right was she?

Anything that Mam said did not remedy her first words, she kissed me right in the forehead and said she was sorry, I kissed her cheek in return as a sign while I was upset, it wasn't with her.

I arrived at the last party of the Holidays still feeling odd, I looked around trying to find someone I knew and I told myself to relax this time around Augusto and I actually made proper plans. No fate bullshit, we wanted to make the effort and be sure to be there at the same time.

Avery texted me a little before saying she was almost ready, apparently she got on with Millie and they were texting each other about the party and Avery had high hopes that today was the day.

The last party was as ridiculous as the other ones of course, but this time I couldn't stop the giggles. It didn't annoy me anymore, not the way it did before.

Elisa Thompson transformed her huge home in a mystery train, complete with the little compartments, a woman with a trolley, and most of the guests dressed in 1920's with pearls and feathers.

The murder mystery party was the crown of an intense week, the cherry on top that I usually threw in the bin but nevertheless this time around I was ready to try.

"You didn't even try, did you?" Avery's voice came to my ear and I turned to find her and Miles dressed head to toe in perfect 20's costumes.

I shrugged, "Costumes are not my thing. You look amazing, Ave."

My best friend smiled big, Miles as usual got us drinks and passed along and we cheered:

"To the first perfect holiday season with our little London with us!" said Avery.

We toasted enthusiastically and I teared up a little. So much had happened that I almost forgot the best part was to be in something they participated every year. I was finally there and they were so happy to share it with me.

"Now…" Avery said straightening herself from

a half hug I gave her, "Where's Millie?"

"The girl should get a restraining order," Miles told me in the second Avery left our side.

I laughed, "What about you and Tania?"

He shook his head, pressing a hand on his heart, "I'm really done with that mess, Lon. It's not healthy, you know? I'm going to look for someone nice, that actually likes me."

I looked at my handsome smart and gentle friend, something told it wouldn't be difficult to find a girl who liked him for who he was.

"Oh look," Miles wiggled his eyebrows to our left and I followed, "Your dude," Like I hadn't seen him.

Augusto parted the crowd with his slow, no rush to get anywhere easy way. It was a way of walking that was only his, a smirk that I couldn't ignore.

My jaw hit the floor, he was actually dressed up, wearing a pinstripe suit and a black bowler hat.

"You're one of them!" I laughed.

"One of them?"

"The dressing up people!"

"Surprise."

"I wouldn't ever have guessed…"

Augusto shook his head slowly, "We have a lot of ground to cover, let's get going…"

CHAPTER TWENTY

"Oreos," I nodded, "Even if I wasn't vegan," I was very sure and when the little red ball came my way I paddled it quickly.

"I have to say cheesecake…"

I made a face, and Augusto asked, "What?"

We were playing ping pong in the back room, a few stoner kids watching us play with one another with vague smiles, which was probably because of the things we were saying more so than the way we were playing.

"Cheesecake… It's a cheese…cake."

"Yes, it's the best of both worlds. Moving on, favourite book?"

"You're asking all the wrong questions. No one cares about that shit, it doesn't mean anything."

"I thought you were a book person!" He exclaimed, hitting the ball with force.

"I am," I lost that point of course, and I got to turn and get the ball from the kids watching us, "But I'm not the books I read or my favourite dessert," I served.

"Alright, I get you, what are you?"

I chuckled, "Too deep!"

"You're indecisive," He told me, getting one more point over me, "and shit at this game."

"My Mam had me when she was only sixteen, so we're very close. My stepfather is one of my favourite people in the world because he is super quiet but he knows shit and I like that. I think everything is political, I hate small talk, I have a strong opinion about everything and I will never judge anyone for anything. It's against my rules."

I finished saying that and Augusto was smiling, enough for me to get a point on him, which made him chuckle.

"Now that's cheating!"

The "train" trolley passed us and Augusto got a handful of snake jellies making me laugh. I was sitting by the bar, having a vodka lime, as usual. Augusto sat on the tall stool beside me and spread his findings:

"Vegan, I know…" He said before I refused anything.

"Mostly grossed out that you are eating from this gross bar…" I laughed.

"Oh, shit, that's true," But he put it all in his mouth. "Antibodies. Good for you."

"So willing to eat nasty bits…" I observed, "I'm so glad we're learning about each other."

"We started so well. I met you and I knew you

hated More than Words…"

I couldn't stop myself from laughing out loud and hoping no one from school heard the joke.

"Let's talk about things we hate, then," I suggested, "There's plenty of things to hate out there."

"I hate watching sports," Augusto said straight out.

"Really?"

"I do… just think about it. You're not doing anything! You're just sitting there shouting at your TV and getting upset for no good reason!"

"Fair enough…" I thought for a second, "I really hate when couples take a long time to get together on a TV show, like we all know is about to happen…"

He laughed and we talked about more stuff we hate, like Augusto's strong hatred for pineapple that met my intense love for all fruits. It was fun and easy and everything you want on a date. So each time I thought how perfect it was, fate or not, meet-cute or not, I got that same cold feeling in the pit of my belly and the echo of Mam's question in my head.

Thankfully, Avery took us to the dance floor at that point and I let her guide us to the centre where Miles We e laughed and goofed around, Augusto played around with my friends like he was one of them. His arms circled around my waist and even through the laughter and jokes floating around it was heard to control the sudden bumping of my heart.

I was in deep shit.

I knew when he made a joke about the way Miles was dancing, I knew when he took my hand and twirled me around. Just complete utterly deep shit of someone that is swooning for a guy that won't stay.

The perfect holiday romance cliché.

When we danced all the songs that were worth dancing, Augusto took me by the hand, guiding me out of the house.

The door closed behind us and my ears rang right after the music stopped. Augusto's hat was long gone but it did nothing to his charm on that suit.

"Which party was the best party?"

"All the themed parties were amazing!" I snickered sitting on the steps in front of us.

"This is definitely my favourite one."

"It's not bad," I shrugged trying my best to look cool but knowing I failed.

"So you're leaving…"

"Tomorrow."

I nodded for lack of anything else to do, and thank god he kept talking, "We're spending Christmas day with Marcela."

"Ok… Don't you think it's odd? That we spent the whole night getting to know each other for what?"

Augusto's reaction was the one I learned to expect of him, the slow and knowing smirk, the calm expression like he knew better than the rest of us. Extending his hand to me he waited until I took and helped me up, "I told you all about the whole meeting with each other all the time. It's like you barely listen."

"I imagine it gets hard when people are in different countries…"

"I'm not worried."

I looked up to him and he didn't look worried at all. Not even a little bit.

I held my breath, his hazel eyes on me. His

hand went up from my hand to my arm and then my waist as I fell forwards to get closer to him.

I knew what was happening but I still felt the surprise when Augusto's lips touched mine and we got as close as we could possibly get.

My hands went up his arms and finally found each other behind his neck, I sighed into him and I felt his smile even while we kissed.

It wasn't long, it felt like just a second and then our kiss slowed down and with a peck on my lips it finally stopped.

"Ok, so that was that," I joked.

"Not bad."

"No… I think…" I shook my head, I had nothing to say about the best kiss of my life, so I asked, "Where are you going to meet your sister?"

The damn all knowing smile made an appearance. "Dublin."

I laughed hard, my head falling on his chest and Augusto.

"I'm not lying," holding me by the waist, "Marcela moved to Dublin a few years ago, she works in a company there."

I shook my head and looked up to him, "So that's how secure you are? That we are going to be meeting so many times, over and over again?"

"Oh, yes, I am sure. I don't know why you're taking so long to understand…"

"I understand… I'm just not sure if I believe it."

His hands squeezed me tight and his nose came down to mine and we breathed each other.

"Tell you what… Next time we see each other,

you can tell me how right I was."

EPILOGUE

My trusted dry cleaners wasn't far from Mam's place and I couldn't wait to see if Maria thought she could rescue the twenty years old dress.

When I opened the door, Maria's daughter Sandra widened her eyes, "Mom! She has it!"

Maria came from the back, parting the curtains of clean clothes to have a look on me. Maria was fierce, kind and I liked her so very much, she was the first one I told about my plans to use Mam's old dress as my wedding dress. Maria was waiting all this time to see the state of the dress to see if she could do something about it.

I rushed myself to the counter and took the blue eggshell dress off the bag and displayed to Maria, "It doesn't look bad, right?"

Maria narrowed her eyes, analysing every inch of the dress, her eyes looking down at the hem and the little embroidered yellow flowers.

"Tell me you can do it, Maria…"

"I can do it," She breathed out, "Because I'm that good, not because this dress is good enough to go down the aisle in."

Sandra and I laughed and my eyes welled up a little. I tried to hide, but Maria wasn't one to prey into my business.

"Ok, leave it with me. Are we adding something? Making it long maybe?"

I made a face, I never thought of changing the dress but if anyone was able to give it a new life that was Maria, she waved me off, "Leave it with me. I can draw something, uh?"

I nodded and jumped up and down from the excitement, "Now you go, I have to work don't I?"

Maria shushed me, I smiled to Sandra who smiled back and something in me just tingled from head to toe.

I left Maria's shop feeling different, like all the stars finally aligned. But again, why wouldn't they?

> London: I got the dress.
> Augusto: Really?
> London: Yeah! I have it here!
> Augusto: Can I see it?
> London: No.
>
> Augusto: ☹
> Augusto: Where are you now?
> London: Just left it with Maria.
> Augusto: I hope it works out, babe.
> Augusto: Bring dinner!
> London: HA! I ate with Mam and Emmet,

loser! Fend for yourself!

I giggled when I finished sending the message knowing he was going to think I was at least entertained by me, before ordering three gigantic burgers if I knew him enough.

Augusto and I met when we were seventeen and we shared a few parties and one single kiss. I was right to assume different countries would make meeting a little difficult, but he was more right than he was wrong.

We met again, and again and again and once more for good measure. Our lives were intertwined from beginning to end, I blinked and there we were, together again in the most crazy ways.

He always found me. Every time, at each turn. His words still rang in my ears, the words he asked once, before we were even a proper we.

"Ok, are you ready?"

"For what?"

"For being together."

I laughed and he laughed with me, and it felt like it was a joke, but Augusto got a job and moved to New York. For two people who always met in random places, we finally never met again. Afterall, you can't meet if you aren't ever apart.

I opened the door of our apartment, Augusto was right in the middle of our sitting room playing video games, when I locked the door, he pressed stop and looked up to me.

"So dress is sorted?"

"Dress is sorted."

The dawn slowest of smiles again, "Are you ready to get married, London Montgomery?"

YAHOLST
Christmas

JAN 1 3 2025
YA

Made in the USA
Las Vegas, NV
01 November 2022